The Longest Night of Charlie Noon

The
Longest
Night
of
Charlie
Noon

CHRISTOPHER EDGE

DELACORTE PRESS

Text copyright © 2019, 2020 by Christopher Edge
Jacket art copyright © 2020 by Jamey Christoph
Interior stick and grid illustrations copyright © 2019 by Christina Edge

All rights reserved. Published in the United States by Delacorte Press, an imprint of Random House Children's Books, a division of Penguin Random House LLC, New York. Originally published in the United Kingdom in paperback and in slightly different form by Nosy Crow, London, in 2019.

Delacorte Press is a registered trademark and the colophon is a trademark of Penguin Random House LLC.

Visit us on the Web! rhcbooks.com

Educators and librarians, for a variety of teaching tools, visit us at
RHTeachersLibrarians.com

Library of Congress Cataloging-in-Publication Data
Names: Edge, Christopher, author.
Title: The longest night of Charlie Noon / Christopher Edge ; interior stick and grid illustrations, Christina Edge.
Description: First American edition. | New York : Delacorte Press, [2020] | "Originally published in the United Kingdom in paperback and in slightly different form by Nosy Crow, London, in 2019." | Audience: Ages 9–12. |
Summary: As time plays tricks and night falls without warning, Johnny, Dizzy, and Charlie, who are lost in the woods, must elude the danger that lurks in shadows and work together to find a way out. Includes note about the science behind the story.
Identifiers: LCCN 2019041092 (print) | LCCN 2019041093 (ebook) |
ISBN 978-0-593-17308-4 (hardcover) | ISBN 978-0-593-17309-1 (library binding) |
ISBN 978-0-593-17310-7 (ebook)
Subjects: CYAC: Lost children—Fiction. | Forests and forestry—Fiction. | Space and time—Fiction. | Adventure and adventurers—Fiction. | Night—Fiction.
Classification: LCC PZ7.E2265 Lon 2020 (print) | LCC PZ7.E2265 (ebook) | DDC [Fic]—dc23

The text of this book is set in 12.75-point Goudy Old Style BT.
Interior design by Stephanie Moss

Printed in the United States of America
10 9 8 7 6 5 4 3 2 1
First American Edition

For anyone who's ever felt lost in the woods.
And for Chrissie, Alex and Josie, as always.

Where am I going? I don't quite know.
What does it matter where people go?
Down to the woods where the blue-bells grow-
Anywhere, anywhere. *I don't know.*

—A. A. Milne, "Spring Morning"

Once upon a time, three kids got lost in the woods.

Sounds like a fairy story, doesn't it?

But what exactly is *a time*?

Is it a second, a minute, an hour or a day? Or are we talking about a week, a month, a year, maybe even a life-time?

The blink of an eye lasts for a tenth of a second, while scientists reckon that the universe is 13.8 billion years old.

Tick.

Tick.

Tick.

Can I tell you a secret?

Once upon a time doesn't exist.

This story starts once upon a *now*.

1

Johnny Baines says there's a monster in here. Dizzy thinks it might be a spy. But as I scramble up the grassy bank of bluebells at the edge of the woods, it's hard to believe there could be anything bad here at all.

Sunlight filters through the trees, bathing the grassy path ahead in shifting patterns of brightness. The faint breeze whispering through the leaves makes their shadows flicker like ripples on an imaginary river that's following the path through the woods.

Dizzy's already striding along, his hiccupping walk making it look like he's forever on the verge of falling over.

"It's this way, Charlie," he says, glancing back to beckon me on. "That's where I saw the first one."

I nod, but I'm in no real hurry to catch up with Dizzy

yet. This is the first time I've been into the woods, and for a moment, I stand absolutely still, slowly filling my senses with this place.

From the back of our school the woods look close enough to touch, a solid bank of forest green that fills half of the horizon. When we set off I thought it would only take us ten minutes to get here, but I hadn't reckoned on the strange zigzagging path that Dizzy took, following the edges of the fields that lie between the village and the woods.

Most of the time we didn't even seem to be walking in the right direction, turning right, then left, then right again, before taking a long detour around the farmhouse that marks the halfway point between the village and the trees. But when I asked Dizzy why we couldn't just walk in a straight line, pointing out the farm track that led to the corner of the woods, he shot me an anxious look.

"You've not met Mr. Jukes, who owns the farm, have you?"

I shook my head. We only moved here from London a couple of months ago. It all happened so fast. Dad lost his job and then Granddad Noon died, leaving us his house in his will. That's when Mum and Dad decided to escape from the city and move back to this tiny village where Dad grew up. I didn't get a say. I just had to do what I was told. I used to have friends in London, but now all I've got is Dizzy.

"He'll fetch the police if he catches you trespassing on his land," Dizzy warned me, casting a nervous glance in the direction of Jukes's farm. "Or set his dog on you."

From behind the long barn came the sound of an angry bark. That was all I needed to hear to make me hurry up. I didn't want to get bitten by some mangy farm animal. I'd probably catch rabies and die. The one thing I've learned since we moved here is that the countryside's full of germs.

So when we finally reached the edge of the woods, scrambling up the bank and out of sight of the farm, I breathed a sigh of relief. I say a sigh of relief, but it was actually more of a gasp, as the walk had left me completely out of breath. All week the weather's been blazing hot, but this is the hottest day yet. It's not even June, but on the news they said if the summer carries on like this, it'll be the hottest since record keeping began.

All I want to do is stop and catch my breath, but Dizzy is still striding ahead.

"Come on," he calls out again.

Dizzy isn't Dizzy's real name, by the way. It's actually Dylan, but everyone calls him Dizzy, even our teacher, Miss James. She says it's because he's got a headful of sky, always staring out the classroom window as he watches the birds fly by.

But right now Dizzy's gaze is fixed firmly to the ground as his lolloping walk takes him deeper into the woods. Not wanting to be left behind, I hurry to catch up.

Trees line the sun-dappled path like sentries, their serried ranks stretching as far as my eye can see. Between the broad trunks I glimpse snatches of purple, white and yellow from the waves of wildflowers that carpet the woodland floor. The air feels warm under the overhanging branches, and the mossy grass puts a spring in my step as I finally catch up with Dizzy.

"So what exactly are we looking for?" I ask.

"A sign," Dizzy replies, glancing up from the path. "Just like I told you I saw."

Dizzy comes to the woods every day after school. He says he's got this special place where he sits to sketch the birds that nest here. Before we moved to the countryside the only birds I ever saw were the pigeons in the park. Flying rats, Dad called them. But the back of Dizzy's schoolbook is filled with drawings of more birds than I even knew there were. Woodpeckers, willow warblers, blackcaps and song thrushes. Dizzy's teaching me their names, pointing them out when they flit overhead as we sit at the edge of the school field.

That was where we were today when he told me what he'd found in the woods. The rest of the class were playing rounders, and I was supposed to be keeping deep field, but I'd gotten bored because nobody was hitting the ball in my direction, so I'd sat down on the grass next to Dizzy.

Dizzy doesn't have to play games because he caught polio when he was little and it made one of his legs shorter than the other. This means Miss James just lets him sit and watch us play, but he spends most of his time drawing birds instead. That's what he was doing when I sat down next to him.

"What are you drawing?" I asked.

"Shhh," Dizzy replied, motioning with his pencil toward the fence at the end of the field.

Following the direction of his pencil tip, I looked up to see a plump reddish-brown bird perched on the fence's top rung.

"What is it?"

"Shhh!" Dizzy whispered again, frowning as he put his pencil to the page. "It's a nightingale."

Keeping my mouth shut, I watched as Dizzy drew, his pencil strokes bringing the bird to life on the page of his exercise book: the thin curve of its beak, the black bead of its eye, the scaly lines of the feathers on its wings kept folded close to its side. It was as though Dizzy could see the shape of the nightingale hidden on the page and was just tracing this invisible outline.

And then the nightingale sang.

It opened its beak wide, and a rich stream of whistles and trills burst out into the sky. I stared at the nightingale, astonished. Another flurry of notes rang out from its beak, even faster than the first—this liquid melody quickly rising to a crescendo. Then the nightingale fell silent, its head bobbing from side to side as if the bird was searching for a reply. But all I could hear was the scratching of Dizzy's pencil.

I glanced down at his drawing of the bird, the nightingale now still on the page, but when I looked up again all I saw was a sudden blur of movement, the real nightingale's wings beating against the sky as it wheeled toward the woods.

Dizzy lifted his face to the sun as he watched the nightingale soar. As it disappeared into the green of the trees, he turned toward me.

"I found something in the woods last night."

Even though the nightingale had flown, Dizzy kept his voice low, as if confiding a secret. From the other end of the field came a distant chorus of "Catch it!" followed by a ragged cheer, and I had to shuffle closer to hear exactly what Dizzy said next.

"I think it might've been left by a spy."

As soon as Dizzy mentioned the word "spy," a picture jumped into my head of the books Dad used to keep on a shelf in the hallway of our old house: *The Secret Agent, The Riddle of the Sands, The Thirty-Nine Steps* and *The Valley of Fear*. I don't have any books of my own, so I used to sneak those stories off the shelf when Dad wasn't looking and take them up to my room. Then, when I was supposed to be asleep, I'd bury my head under the covers to read them with a flashlight, taking shelter in their tales of foreign spies and sinister crimes as I tried to ignore the angry words thudding through the walls as Mum and Dad argued downstairs.

"What did you find?" I asked Dizzy, my brain already filling with thoughts of secret documents and stolen gold.

Closing his exercise book, Dizzy looked at me solemnly.

"Sticks," he said, "on the path through the woods."

I couldn't stop myself from laughing.

"Dizzy—it's the woods. Of course there're sticks dropped on the path. What's so strange about that?"

Dizzy's cheeks seemed to darken slightly, his light-brown skin taking on a coppery hue.

"These sticks weren't dropped," he said, stuffing his exercise book back inside his school bag. "They were *arranged*."

"What do you mean 'arranged'?" I asked, still puzzled as to why Dizzy thought a spy was leaving sticks in the woods.

"They were laid out in patterns," Dizzy replied, pushing his school bag to one side. "Some pointing like arrows, others arranged into squares, like a sign. I couldn't help but notice them. Every stick looked exactly the same—all smooth and white—with the bark stripped off each one. The patterns they made looked like some kind of secret code, just like a spy would use."

That got my attention. Since we moved into Grand-dad's old house, the only book I've found to read is one that was left on the shelf in my new bedroom. It's called *Scouting for Boys* and I think it used to belong to my dad. It's all about the skills you need to be a Boy Scout, like making fires and following tracks. In it, there's this story about how some soldiers left secret messages near landmarks like trees to keep them hidden from the enemy. Maybe that's what Dizzy has found.

"Where exactly did you see this?" I asked.

"If we went into the woods after school I could show you," Dizzy said. "Maybe together we could work out what the secret message means."

"What secret message?"

The sound of Johnny Baines's voice caused Dizzy's face to freeze in fear. Then Johnny thudded down on the grass between us, his sudden arrival forcing me to shuffle out of the way of his sharp elbows.

"What message?" Johnny asked again, grabbing hold of Dizzy's bag and tipping its contents onto the grass as if thinking he'd find the answer there. He leaned forward, his broad shoulders hunched as he started to pick through Dizzy's possessions: schoolbooks, pencils and pens, a pair of binoculars and a pocket flashlight. Johnny threw them all to one side, not caring where they landed.

"Hey!" I called out indignantly.

But Johnny just ignored me, turning instead toward Dizzy, who was already cringing in anticipation.

"Come on, birdbrain. Spit it out. What are you hiding from me?"

"I—I found something in the woods," Dizzy stammered,

his words stumbling over each other as if frightened to go first. "There were these sticks laid out on the path—all arranged into shapes in some kind of code. Charlie and I are going to find it again after school. I—we—think it might be a secret message that's been left by a spy."

Johnny screwed up his eyes, squinting into the sun as if trying to decide if Dizzy was telling the truth. Then he laughed out loud.

"That's not a spy," Johnny said, turning toward me with a creepy grin that made my stomach turn. "That's Old Crony."

I wanted to tell Johnny to get lost and leave us alone. I can talk to him like that, even though he's bigger than me. Everyone says Johnny Baines is the toughest kid in school, but he doesn't scare me.

However, there was something in Johnny's know-it-all tone that stopped me from telling him to sling his hook straight away.

"Who's Old Crony?" I asked instead.

Behind Johnny, Dizzy had started to shove his stuff back into his bag. At my question he looked up in alarm, his eyes silently pleading with me to make Johnny go away. But Johnny just stretched his legs out, making himself more comfortable as he started to explain.

"Old Crony lives in the woods. Deep in the heart of the woods. He's been there for years. He'll be the one that's left that message, not some stupid spy."

Beneath the dark line of his close-cropped hair, Johnny's eyes shone with a strange fascination.

"Old Crony eats children, you know."

Dizzy flinched.

"Any kids that cross into his territory are fair game for eating," Johnny continued, his words laced with a grisly delight. "My dad told me that. He says he used to leave any scraps of meat he couldn't sell at the edge of the woods to keep Old Crony quiet."

Johnny's dad runs the butcher's shop in the village. That's why Johnny's sweat stinks of sausages. I think all he ever eats is meat. But he's not scaring me with this fairy tale.

"That's rubbish," I said scornfully. "If Old Crony is real, where does he live? In a house made of gingerbread in the middle of the woods?"

"No," Johnny replied, cocking his head as he fixed me with a dead-eyed stare. "He builds his house out of the bones of the children he catches. Right after he boils them up. Old Crony left those signs to lure you deeper into the woods. I reckon you're next for the pot."

I didn't blink as I held Johnny's stare, wanting to show him that he didn't scare me.

"You're making it up."

"How do *you* know?" Johnny hawked up phlegm and spat a dirty yellow globule onto the grass near my feet. "You've only been here for five minutes. My family's lived here for hundreds of years. We know stuff about the woods. More than you and birdbrain here could ever know."

From across the field came a shrill blast. At the sound of the teacher's whistle, Johnny slowly pulled himself to his feet. He stared down at me, his stocky frame blocking most of the sun.

"If you go into the woods, Old Crony will get you," he said. "You just see."

I glance up now at the maze of branches overhead, scraps of blue still visible between their patchwork of leaves. Then I drop my gaze to the grassy track, cobbles of light and shade marking the path between the trees as Dizzy leads us on.

That's what we're doing. We're going into the woods.

2

"So where exactly did you see it?"

I've asked this question more than a dozen times, but Dizzy just shakes his head again.

"I'm not sure," he says, scratching his thatch of black hair as a frown furrows his brow. He points ahead to where the track splits in two, the path smeared with patches of sunlight as it branches off to the left and to the right. "I thought it was here, near the end of the Walk, but I'm not so sure now."

The paths through the woods have all got different names: the Walk, the Green Trench, the Plumber's Track or something like that. Dizzy's been telling me their names as we've searched in vain for this secret message. He says he's got a map of the woods in his head, so we don't have to worry about getting lost, but as I stare ahead at the forking paths, all looking almost identical beneath the overhanging branches, I don't quite share his confidence.

I glance down at my watch. Beneath the brown leather strap, there's a grubby smear round my wrist, but the vertical hands on the watch face tell me the time.

It's six o'clock.

We've been following this path for more than an hour, but we haven't been able to find a trace of the strange signs that Dizzy says he found here. It's not that we haven't been able to find any sticks. They're everywhere we look. The grassy track is littered with twigs and broken branches that lie where they've fallen. But there's no sign that any spy or even Old Crony has arranged these to spell out some secret code.

To my left, a sudden screech almost makes me jump out of my skin.

Spinning round, I peer into the dense thicket, the tangled web of bramble and bracken completely hiding whatever has made this unearthly sound.

The screeching noise comes again, closer this time, freezing my blood.

I turn toward Dizzy, the worst fears that have lurked in the back of my mind ever since Johnny told us about Old Crony now rushing into the light.

"What is it?" I ask, unable to keep the rising panic out of my voice.

But Dizzy just smiles as a brownish blur erupts out of the undergrowth, its wings flapping into the air before it lands in a clumsy flurry on an overhanging branch.

"It's just a jay," Dizzy says, raising his gaze to peer up at the fawn-colored bird, its black-and-white wings fringed with a dusting of blue.

From its perch, the jay peers down at me, the pale streaked crest of its head darting from side to side as if showing its disapproval. Then it opens its beak wide with another ear-piercing screech, sending a shiver down my spine.

It's just a bird.

My heart's racing; my legs ache; the sweat that has stuck the shirt to my back has turned to a cold clamminess. I thought that coming here with Dizzy was going to be fun—a chance to solve the mystery in the woods—but it's turned into a wild-goose chase.

The jay screeches again, a warning call telling us to go away. Maybe that's what we should do. Maybe it's time to go home.

Mum and Dad think I've gone to Dizzy's house for tea, but they'll be expecting me back soon. Dad will be sitting at the kitchen table, staring at the clock and listening for my key in the lock. The only way I'll be able to tell what kind of mood he's in will be to count the number of empty bottles on the table in front of him. And if there are too many, that's when the shouting will start.

Noisily flapping its tail feathers, the jay hops from its perch on to a higher branch, hiding behind a curtain of leaves as it lets out another angry screech. And then, from the darkness of the undergrowth, I hear a twig snapping.

Still feeling on edge, I peer anxiously into the green twilight that lurks between the trees, but I can't make out the source of the sound. All I can hear now is the constant rustling of leaves, the same sound that has followed us like footsteps through the woods.

I'm sick and tired of this stupid place. I've had enough of playing spies with Dizzy.

"Maybe we should head back now," I say.

But Dizzy doesn't answer, and as I turn around, I see him hurrying ahead, his lolloping stride taking him to the spot where the track splits in two.

"Charlie—over here!" he calls out.

Hurrying to catch up, I almost trip over a half-submerged tree root but manage to stop myself before I fall. When I reach the shade of the tree that stands at the fork in the track, Dizzy is waiting for me.

"What is it?"

Unable to hide the excitement on his face, Dizzy motions down at the ground.

"I found this."

At the base of the tree, a rough circle has been swept, clearing away the leaves and twigs that litter the ground elsewhere. And in the center of this rough circle, three

sticks have been arranged in the shape of an arrow pointing down the left-hand track.

Beneath the overhanging branches the air feels sti-
flingly hot. Sweat stings my eyes as I stare down at the sign.
I wipe my forehead with the back of my sleeve, the thrill of
this discovery rubbing out all thoughts of heading home.

"You were telling the truth," I say, suddenly realizing
that I didn't really believe Dizzy until now.

Shucking his school bag from his shoulder, Dizzy
crouches down next to the arrangement of sticks. Reaching inside his bag, he pulls out a pencil and his notebook,
flicking through it until he finds a blank page.

"What are you doing?" I ask as Dizzy starts to draw.
A trilling call cascades from the branches above us, but I
don't know why Dizzy has to start bird-watching now. Not
now that we've found what we've been searching for.

But then I see that instead of drawing a bird, Dizzy is
actually sketching the sign.

"If this is a secret code, we've got to work out what it
means," he says.

"I think it's pretty obvious what it means." I look at the

arrow on the ground and then straight ahead in the direction that it's pointing. "It's telling us which way to go."

Under the shafts of sunlight breaking through leaves, the path ahead looks almost golden now. A butterfly flits between these sun-dappled patches, its purple wings shimmering as it settles on a leafy bush before taking to the air again. As my eyes follow its flight, I see another patch of scuffed ground farther along the path.

"Look!"

This time I get there first. I peer down to see three sticks laid out on the ground.

I can't really tell which direction this triangle is pointing. Back the way we came? Or into one of the thickets of bramble that lie on either side of the track? The points of the triangle give us three choices, but how can we tell which is the right one? If someone is leaving us directions, then it looks like they want us to get lost.

As Dizzy starts to sketch this new sign, I look around, hoping to find another clue. Countless sticks and twigs are scattered across the track, but my gaze snags on a patch of ground where another rough circle has been swept clear, two sticks left in the center of it. And beyond this I can see yet another arrangement of sticks, lurking in the shade of a nearby tree.

"There's more!"

I hurry over to inspect the first of these new clues, Dizzy trailing in my wake.

An arrow, a triangle and now what looks like a T-junction. It's almost like someone's leaving road signs on the path through the woods.

"What's this supposed to mean?" Dizzy asks, frowning as he marks the sign down in his sketchbook.

"I don't know," I reply, mopping the sweat from my fore-head again, "but it tells us that we're on the right track. Come on."

The next sign is even closer than the last: three sticks laid out in the shade of a huge oak tree.

This one looks like a box with a missing lid, but no clue has been left inside to help us solve this secret code.

Above our heads comes a sudden hushing of leaves, the treetops swaying with leathery creaks. But down here I can't feel any breeze, and the suffocating heat is making it difficult for me to put my thoughts in order. It's as though the air in the woods isn't working properly, starving my brain of the oxygen I need to work out what this means.

I look around, scanning the track for more clues, but all I can see is the usual litter of twigs. Beneath the tunnel of leaves, dappled light swirls along the path like reflections on a river, but beyond that, the thick ferns and bushes straggle into shadow. No more clues to be found.

"This is the last one," I say.

Dizzy is crouching down again, adding this final sign to his sketchbook, but as he looks up from the page a frown furrows his brow.

"These sticks look different from the ones I saw yesterday," he says, his lips pursed as if he's trying to work something out. "Those sticks had their bark stripped clean away, leaving them all smooth and white, but these just look like ordinary sticks."

I shrug.

"Maybe the spy was in a hurry this time."

Dizzy looks doubtful.

"What if it's not a spy?"

"What do you mean?" I say as fresh beads of sweat run down my face. "That's who you said it was."

A frown still creases Dizzy's forehead as he rises to his feet. He hoicks his bag back onto his shoulder, the book still open in his hand

"I only said that's who I thought it might be, but what if Johnny's right? What if it's Old Crony?"

Above our heads, another rustling sound hushes through the leaves. I glance anxiously toward the trunk of the ancient tree, the rough bark cracked and marked with wartlike burrs. In the shadows cast by the swaying leaves it almost looks like the face of a scary old man.

Despite the heat, I shiver, then force out a laugh to disguise my involuntary shudder.

"Johnny was just making that up," I say, looking around to reassure myself. "There's no crazy old man who lives in the woods. Old Crony doesn't exist."

I hold out my hand for Dizzy's book, eager to change the subject.

"Let me have a look."

Dizzy hands the book over and I look down at his sketches of the sticks that we've found.

"What do you think it means, Charlie?"

I frown, trying to make sense of the strange symbols on the page. In Dad's spy novels, the hero is usually able to crack a secret code by finding a codebook or discovering a key that unlocks the mystery. This might be a special word or phrase that suddenly makes sense of everything. In *The Thirty-Nine Steps*, Hannay—the hero—discovers a black book that belonged to a murdered man, filled with what looks like random numbers. But each number corresponds to a letter of the alphabet, and by using a key word to decipher this code, Hannay uncovers the secret of the Black Stone, a deadly group of spies plotting to steal the plans for war.

Sweat rolls down my face, the shade here at the foot of the tree providing little relief from the sweltering heat. My head aches as I stare at the meaningless patterns on the page. I don't have a codebook, and thinking about black stones isn't going to help me solve the mystery of these sticks.

As I shake my head, tiny beads of sweat drip into my eyes with a sudden stinging sensation. My vision blurs, but as I blink, something shifts in my brain, the blurred image turning the shapes that the sticks have made into letters in my mind.

I point to the first of Dizzy's sketches.

"What if this isn't an arrow, but the letter 'E' instead?" I move my finger along the page. "And this triangle of sticks could be an 'A.' That would make this a 'T,' and these sticks at the end might be in the shape of the letter 'U.'"

I look up at Dizzy, my eyes shining with excitement.

"Maybe it's not a code after all. Maybe whoever has left these sticks has written their message in plain English."

Dizzy looks confused.

"But that doesn't spell anything."

For a second my heart sinks, and I think I must have made a mistake. I look down at the page again, trying to work out how I've gotten this wrong.

"E—A—T—U," I say, the sound of the letters turning to words as I speak them out loud. "Eat you."

I look at Dizzy, his face filling with horror as we both realize what this means.

And that's when the monster bursts out of the trees.

3

The monster is shrouded in bloodstained rags, its arms outstretched as it lets loose an earsplitting howl.

Above our heads, the treetops shake as birds flee their perches, ricocheting off the branches in terror as the monster howls again.

The same terror roots me to the spot. I stand frozen, staring in horror at this shambling nightmare made real.

Johnny Baines was telling the truth.

This is Old Crony.

He's come to get us.

I turn toward Dizzy, his mouth opening wide as he screams a single word.

"Run!"

Old Crony stands between us and the way we came. No

way past his flailing arms, and if we stay on the path, we're easy prey. With a split second to decide, there's only one way to go.

Spinning on my heels, I turn and run into the trees.

Ducking beneath the branches, I crash through the undergrowth, my heart thudding in my chest as I plunge into this shadowy world. Tangles of brambles appear out of the gloom, making me swerve as I dive between these clumps of shrubbery. My shoes slide into a swathe of wildflowers, their nodding heads obliterated beneath my pell-mell feet as I blunder wildly on. In the dim green twilight, the woods seem to stretch on forever.

Behind me, I hear the sound of someone else crashing through the undergrowth, but don't dare glance back to see if this is Dizzy following my trail. Then the sound of a triumphant howl, even closer now, gives me the answer I dreaded.

Old Crony's coming to get me.

My chest heaves as I hurdle a fallen tree trunk, my shoes almost slipping on the furry moss that carpets the ground. I take a sharp turn, dodging between a brake of trees, hoping that their maze of twisting branches will shield me from the monster's sight.

I can't hear the sound of birds anymore, just the whiplash crack of snapping branches as I thrash my way through the thicket. Thorns tear at my hands as I claw my way deeper into the woods. I can feel my blood drumming wildly in my ears, each breath coming in a juddering gasp.

Breaking free of the thicket, I glimpse a flash of red beneath my feet, then cry out in alarm as I realize it's a fox, half buried beneath the leaves. But the fox doesn't bolt at my cry, and as a cloud of buzzing flies rises from its moldering fur, I quickly realize why. Beneath its shroud of leaves, the dead fox's sightless eyes stare into mine as if warning me that I'm next.

I stumble on, the sharp pain of a stitch stabbing at my side. Behind me I hear the sound of more branches breaking, a fusillade of cracks that tells me the monster is closing in. Fear rising in my throat, I glance back to see Old Crony emerging from the trees.

I can't breathe. He's so close now. Close enough for me to see the faded bloodstains on the rags that are wrapped around him like a shroud. Inside my head I hear Johnny Baines say *Old Crony eats children, you know.*

I didn't believe him then. I do now.

"Dizzy!" I shout, desperate for help, but the only sound I hear in reply is another whooping howl from this shambling creature that's hunted me down.

My heart hammers in my throat. I should've stayed on the path. This is Old Crony's territory. And I'm for the pot.

Old Crony reaches for me, his grubby fingers emerging from the folds of his bloodstained robes.

Twisting away to evade his grasp, I turn to flee. Beneath the smothering roof of leaves I feel as though I'm drowning in an ocean of green, snatching one last gasping breath before Old Crony drags me under. I kick, trying to outrun this monster on my trail, but instead trip over a fallen branch, my foot snagged by its tangle of ivy.

I pitch forward, my hands clawing at thin air as I fall. For a moment, time seems to expand, a split second stretching out as the ground rises to meet me. Beneath the leaf mold I catch a glimpse of gray stone and I know this is going to hurt. Turning my head, I'm caught in a stray beam of sunlight as I hear a voice calling out my name.

"Charlie!"

Then a sharp pain blooms in the side of my head and the lights go out.

4

"Charlie."

The voice seems to be coming from a long way away.

"Charlie—are you OK?"

There's a brightness filling my vision, squiggled lines of red and black traced against this pinkish glare.

It hurts. The pain a blinding sharpness that seems to fill my brain, but as I open my eyes, it feels sharpest at the side of my head.

Dizzy's face swims into view, framed by a halo of leaves. Sweat shines from his skin, his dark-brown eyes wide with worry.

"Take it easy," he says as I try to sit up. "You fell over and knocked yourself out."

Then a second face appears at Dizzy's shoulder, this one swathed in tattered, bloodstained rags.

Old Crony.

I shout out in alarm, my head spinning as I scramble backward in fear.

But then Old Crony reaches up to pull these rags away and I see instead Johnny Baines's pink, sweaty face staring back at me.

"It was you!" I shout, this sudden realization unleashing a surge of anger deep inside me. "Not Old Crony!"

For a second I forget about the pain that's pounding in my brain as I stagger to my feet. I launch myself at Johnny, ready to punch his lights out. But before I can even reach him, the trees begin to spin as a fresh firework of pain explodes behind my eyes.

I feel myself pitching forward again, but this time Dizzy catches me before I fall.

"You're bleeding," he says, helping me into a sitting position with my back resting against an upturned tree stump.

I reach my hand up to my head, to the place where the firework pain feels brightest, and feel the wetness there. It's getting dark now inside the woods, but when I look down at my fingers, the sticky redness there seems even darker. This isn't sweat—it's blood.

"Help me," Dizzy says, glancing back at Johnny, who's still standing there openmouthed.

Dizzy's words seem to jolt Johnny out of his trance. Shucking off the rags he's still got wrapped around him, he grudgingly tears off a strip.

"You can use this as a bandage," he says, holding out the grubby piece of material.

As Dizzy reaches out to take it, I shake my head even though this makes the trees start spinning again.

"You can't use that," I protest, even as my vision runs red.

"We don't have anything else," Dizzy says, looking really worried now as the blood drips into my eyes. "Hold still."

I don't have any choice except to do what he says, trying not to faint as Dizzy first cleans the wound with his handkerchief before wrapping the bandage around me. The pressure of this makes my head pound even harder, but as Dizzy binds the ends of the bandage together, I realize that it seems to have stopped the bleeding.

"That'll have to do for now," Dizzy says as he takes a step back. "But you'll need to get your mum to put some antiseptic on when you get home."

Johnny's still standing there, watching me, the corners of his mouth curling into a smile.

"What's so funny?" I snap, struggling to keep a lid on my anger as my head pounds.

"You should've seen your face," Johnny says with a smirk, glancing down at the bloodstained rags now dumped in a bundle at his feet. "My dad uses these to keep the floor clean when he's butchering animals for the shop, but they had you fooled I was Old Crony, didn't they?"

I sniff, realizing now where the strange sausagey smell is coming from. Fighting back the urge to throw up, I pull myself to my feet.

"You're an idiot," I say, as the trees start to sway around me again. I grab hold of the tree stump, waiting for this dizziness to pass, but Johnny doesn't seem to care.

"You're the idiots for believing in fairy stories," he sneers.

In the dimming light, the shadows surrounding Johnny seem to blur. I take a deep breath, getting ready to tell him to get lost, but it's Dizzy who speaks up instead.

"It's not a fairy story," he says. "We found the secret message on the path."

Johnny looks at Dizzy and laughs.

"I know what you found," he says, speaking deliberately slowly, as if to emphasize every word. "Who do you think left those broken sticks there?"

Dizzy's face falls, but this only seems to amuse Johnny more.

"You're a couple of babies," he laughs.

"Get lost," I shout, finally able to get my words out. "You're the baby, dressing up like some make-believe monster and creeping round the woods. Don't you have any *real* friends to play with?"

This wipes the grin off Johnny's face. He steps toward me, his hands clenching into fists.

"Who'd want to be friends with you?" He glances across at Dizzy, then looks back at me. "The cripple and the freak. You might as well both stay in the woods where you belong. I'm going home."

With that, Johnny turns on his heel, twigs crunching beneath his feet as he stomps off in search of the path. I watch him go, the tree trunks and scrubby branches gradually blurring him out of focus as he disappears into the growing gloom.

"I think he's heading the wrong way," Dizzy says.

"Good."

I glance down at my watch, wanting to find out exactly what time it is. The hour and the minute hand are both stuck pointing downward, telling me its half past six, but the second hand that should be ticking on is stuck there too. It must have stopped.

I try winding the watch, but the hands refuse to move. It must have gotten broken when I fell. Something else to explain to Mum and Dad, along with the bloodstains on my shirt and the bandage wrapped round my head. I'm going to be in so much trouble.

I look up. The light seems to be failing, the scattered patches of sky I can see now tinged with pink and orange. Dusk is slowly seeping through the leaves, filling the woods with a rising darkness. It feels much later than half past six.

In my mind, I can see Dad sitting at the kitchen table, more empty bottles lined up in front of him now as he watches the clock go round. The jangling pain beneath my bandage makes me feel sick to my stomach. It's time to face the music.

"Come on," I say to Dizzy. "Let's go home."

5

I pick my way through the undergrowth, searching in vain for a glimpse of the path.

It's getting more difficult now to see where the shadows end and the trees begin, the twisting maze of trunks and branches merging to form a vague darkness. Even the colors seem to be fading from the flowers that carpet the woodland floor, their nodding heads blurring into shadows.

The pain in my head has now dulled to a nagging ache, but as Dizzy's lolloping footsteps crunch through the leaves behind me, I don't know if I can keep going for much longer. Blocking the way ahead is a fallen tree, its toppled trunk lying crashed amid the dense thicket. No sign of any way round this.

Part of me just wants to sit down until my head stops

hurting, but as the darkness descends most of me just wants to find the way out of this stupid wood. I flinch as another twig cracks beneath my feet, the sound as loud as a gunshot. From the bushes and shrubs comes a constant rustling sound, the tic-tac of tiny animal feet scuttling through the brambles. We need to press on.

I clamber over the fallen trunk, the bark beneath my fingers waxy to the touch. As I take my hand away I see with a sudden rush of alarm that my fingers are stained rust-red. Worried, I lift my hand to my head as Dizzy clambers over the tree behind me.

"I'm bleeding again," I say, holding out my hand to show him.

Dizzy peers at me through the gloom, then shakes his head reassuringly.

"That's not blood," he says, holding up his hands to show me that his own palms are stained red too. "It's just the lichen that's growing on the tree."

I glance down at the fallen trunk, noticing now the rust-red moss that's growing there. This is why I hate the countryside. Even the trees are trying to make me think that I'm bleeding to death.

Feeling relieved, I look around, trying to work out which way to go now. There's no clear path ahead, only crooked inky tracks that quickly straggle into darkness. A sour, weedy smell hangs in the air, and I can't remember now why I thought this was the right way to go.

As if reading my mind, Dizzy peers into the gloom.

"Are you sure this is the right way?" he asks.

"I don't know," I snap, unable to hide my irritation. "I thought it was right because you were following me. You said you had a map of these woods in your head." I point to the bandage that's wrapped around mine. "I wasn't paying much attention to which way I was going when I thought Old Crony was chasing me."

I can't stop myself from shivering at the memory.

"There are more than sixty miles of paths and tracks through these woods." Dizzy frowns. "We've got to make sure we find the right one."

He looks back over his shoulder, past the fallen tree.

"Maybe we should've followed Johnny."

I shake my head, this movement generating a fresh jangle of pain inside my brain. Following Johnny was the last thing I wanted to do. He's the reason we're in this mess.

"You said he was heading the wrong way," I say, remembering what Dizzy said as we watched Johnny stomp off into the trees.

"I thought he was," Dizzy says, scratching his head as he looks around again. "But this doesn't look at all like I remember it. I thought we'd have reached the Walk by now and we'd be able to follow the path back out of the woods."

I peer down the twisted tracks, trying to decide which one looks like it will lead us home. Then I hear a sudden crack, followed by the sound of splintering wood.

Something's moving through the trees.

I turn toward Dizzy in fear as the splintering sound comes again. It sounds like some wild animal is hurrying toward us, crashing through the undergrowth as it sniffs us out.

Dizzy is staring straight ahead with a desperate look. Following his gaze, I see the nearest tree begin to reach toward us, its low branches cracking as whatever's pushing them forward draws near. I hold my breath, waiting to confront whatever monster is out there, thoughts of Old Crony crowding into my head.

And then Johnny Baines blunders through the trees.

He comes to a sudden halt, staring at us in surprise.

"I can't find the path," he gasps, his sweaty face now grimed with dirt. "I've been searching for ages, but there's no sign of it anywhere."

His white shirt and black shorts are matted with dust, like he's just been rolling through the leaves. Beneath the scabs on his knees, his legs are scratched and bleeding, mud splattered across the tops of his shoes.

It's not a monster. It's only Johnny. And he looks even worse than me.

I remember how to breathe again, letting out a sigh of relief.

"You went the wrong way," I say, allowing myself a small smile at the state that Johnny's in. "Isn't that right, Dizzy?"

But Dizzy just looks confused.

"How did you get ahead of us?" he asks, peering in the direction that Johnny's just come from.

"I don't know," Johnny replies, wiping the sweat from his forehead with a grubby sleeve. "I thought you were following me. I couldn't find the path, so I doubled back, and I caught my foot in a rabbit hole and fell over." He pauses for a second, catching his breath after this flurry of words. "It feels like I've been walking for hours."

That's ridiculous. Johnny only left us ten minutes ago. He must've hit his head too if he thinks he's been gone for hours.

"You must have walked round in a circle," I tell him. "We've been walking in the opposite direction to you. And you've only been gone for a few minutes. Tell him, Dizzy."

But Dizzy doesn't reply, and I glance across to see him staring up into the trees.

"What is it?"

Lowering his gaze, Dizzy meets mine, a look of real worry on his face.

"It shouldn't be this dark yet," he says quietly.

I look up. Shadowy branches scrape against the sky, but there's a ragged hole in the roof of leaves where the tree has fallen. And the patch of sky I can see through this isn't blue but gray.

I look down at my watch, forgetting for a second that it's broken. The hands still say it's half past six, but above our heads the sky has turned to slate.

This can't be right. We've only been in the woods for a couple of hours or so. The sun doesn't set until nine o'clock, and it can't be near that time yet. Can it? Beneath the bandage, my head aches. How long was I knocked out?

"Maybe the sun's stuck behind a really thick cloud," I say, trying to make sense of the failing light. "It just looks darker because we're in the woods."

Dizzy shakes his head.

"Listen."

Standing completely still, I angle my head to try to catch the sound that Dizzy seems to want me to hear. But there's nothing. All I can hear is silence.

I glance across at Johnny and see the same puzzlement on his face.

"I can't hear anything," I say.

"That's what I mean," Dizzy replies. "The birds have stopped singing."

"So what?" Johnny pipes up. "Worried it's getting too dark for you to do one of your stupid drawings?"

"No," Dizzy says, ignoring the sneer in Johnny's question. "The birds know what time it is. They must be roosting in their nests now. That's why they've stopped singing. They're telling us that it's night."

Like the darkness, the silence is thickening around us as Dizzy speaks, swallowing his words.

I strain my ears, desperate to hear something that will prove him wrong. It's not just that the birds have stopped singing, but that the woods themselves are hushed. The constant rustling of leaves is now stilled to a noiseless roar. I shiver, a cold sweat soaking the bandage that's wrapped round my head.

Instinctively, Dizzy, Johnny and I draw closer to each other, the crunch of dry leaves beneath our feet unnaturally loud in the silence.

Then a loud churring call rings from the trees, the trilling notes tumbling over each other in a torrent of clicks.

Chk—chk—chk—chk—tshrr—chk—chk—chk—chk.

"That's a bird," I say, unable to hide my relief as I look up in search of the sound. "You see—it can't be night yet."

Above my head the shadowy branches reach into the silvered darkness as, from its hidden perch, the bird calls out again.

Chk—chk—chk—tshrr—tshrr.

"That's a nightjar," Dizzy says, keeping his voice low. "It's a nocturnal bird."

"What do you mean 'nocturnal'?" Johnny asks, his voice much louder than Dizzy's. "It's still a bird, isn't it?"

"Yes," Dizzy replies, "but one that only comes out at night. That's when it goes hunting for food."

I don't want to believe what Dizzy's telling us. I told Mum and Dad that I'd be back by half past seven. But even as the nightjar sings, shadows have worn away the edges of everything. The gathering darkness is closing in, and I realize with a shudder that he's right.

It's night and we're lost in the woods.

The nightjar calls again, its song sounding stranger than before.

Tshrr—chk—tshrr—chk. Tshrr—tshrr—tshrr.

Its call seems to be slowing down, the blurred churring of notes stretching out into individual sounds, each one louder than the last.

"That bird's getting on my nerves," Johnny growls. Bending down, he picks something off the ground and, as he straightens up, I see that he's got a stone in his hand.

"Don't—"

But before Dizzy can even finish his sentence Johnny launches the stone high into the tree, aiming it straight at the source of the sound.

Tshrr—tshrr—chk.

I hear the fizz of the stone as it rips through the leaves, followed by a clunk. The bird falls silent and, for a second, I think that maybe the stone has hit home.

"That's shut it up," Johnny says, dusting his hands in satisfaction.

Chk—tshrr. Chk—chk—chk.

The hairs prick up on the back of my neck—the eerie call is now coming from directly overhead. It doesn't even sound like a bird anymore, more like some kind of machine. All I can hear are the same two notes—one short and one long—repeating in ever-shifting patterns.

As this rhythmic clicking worms its way into my head, I realize, with a sudden rush, what it is.

"This isn't birdsong—it's Morse code!"

In Dad's old book about scouting there's a whole page about Morse code. It's a special code that uses dots and dashes to send messages. Every letter in the alphabet has its own set of dots and dashes. And when you use a Morse key to send a message in Morse code, these dots and dashes sound like clicks—just like the ones I can hear now.

Chk—tshrr.

Dot—dash.

"How can a bird be singing in Morse code?" Johnny says, sneering at me out of the shadows. "You must've lost your marbles when you hit your head."

I shoot Johnny an angry stare, my glare almost lost in the gloom. I know what Morse code sounds like.

I found an old-fashioned Morse key when I was clearing Granddad's stuff out of the cupboard under the eaves in my new bedroom. It was mounted on a wooden base with the words "PROPERTY OF THE POST OFFICE" stamped on the front. Granddad used to work at the village post office, so I think he must've nicked it from there. How it works is really simple. The main part of the Morse key is a long brass lever with a round wooden knob at one end. Then beneath the lever there's a coiled spring and two metal contacts—one at the top and one at the bottom. When you push down the lever, the two contacts click together, closing the circuit and sending a signal. One click for a dot, with the lever held down three times longer to make a dash.

In *Scouting for Boys* it says that every scout ought to learn Morse code so they can send messages in the wild. Even though Dad says I can't be a scout, I still practiced with the Morse key until I knew the code by heart. I'd sit at the desk in my bedroom, tapping out secret messages to try to drown out the sound of Mum and Dad arguing downstairs, every click a secret wish that someone would send a message back, telling me how to escape.

From the trees comes the same Morse-code clicking, even louder than before. As I listen it seems as if the same patterns keep repeating, halting flurries of clicks and churrs filling the darkness with sound.

Chk—chk. Tshrr—chk.

Johnny's sneering question echoes in my mind. *How can a bird be singing in Morse code?* But as a cold sweat runs down my neck, I suddenly realize that that isn't the right question.

I turn toward Dizzy.

"Quick," I say. "I need something to write with."

Still looking confused, Dizzy bends down in reply. Reaching inside his bag, he pulls out his exercise book and a pencil and hands them over to me.

"What do you need to write?"

"If this is Morse code, then we can work out what it's saying." I flick through the pages of the exercise book, sketches of birds flitting by in the gloom. "I can decode the message."

Finding a blank page, I crouch with the book on my lap, pencil ready to catch every click of the code.

Chk—tshrr. Chk—chk—chk.

As I listen to the clicks and churrs, my hand translates them into dots and dashes on the page, a beat of silence marking time between each flurry of sound.

"This is stupid," Johnny says, his voice suddenly loud as he peers over my shoulder. "What kind of message do you think a bird's going to be sending? 'Get away from my tree'?"

Ignoring Johnny, I strain my ears so I don't miss a single sound. Each one is marked with a dot or dash on the page, even though I can barely see these in the semi-darkness. The mechanical notes seem to be stretching out, their odd echoes bouncing round the trees. It's as though the woods are some giant Morse-code machine that's slowly breaking down.

Chk—chk. Tshrr—chk. Tshrr—tshrr—CHK!

This final noise is so loud it sounds like a tree falling, a splintering crack that makes me jump in surprise while Johnny swears out loud.

"What the hell was that?"

The pencil trembles in my hand as I wait for what comes next, but nothing comes. Only silence.

"It's stopped."

I look up from the page and then cry out in surprise as a bright light almost blinds me.

"What the—"

"Sorry," Dizzy says as the light dips. Blinking, I wait for the blotches to fade from my eyes before I see that Dizzy is holding a flashlight. Its yellow beam is now pointing at the exercise book, still open on my knees. "I thought you might need a bit of light."

Still blinking, I look around—the darkness that surrounds us now is as complete as the silence that fills the woods again. Then I look down at the exercise book, the flashlight illuminating the marks on the page.

.- ... - --- .-. -- .. ... -.-. --- -- .. -. --.

Remembering the code I learned by heart, I start to scribble the right letters beneath the dots and dashes.

Dot—dash.

A

Dot—dot—dot.

S

Dash.

T

Dash—dash—dash.

O

My hand trembles as I write down the rest of the letters, the message making no sense until I reach the end of the line.

"So what does it say, then?" Johnny asks.

My heart thumps in my chest as I check the code again, wanting to make sure I've not made a mistake. But I haven't.

I look up from the book, the yellow flashlight beam wobbling slightly as Dizzy and Johnny wait for my reply. I take a deep breath before I speak, the sound sharp in the silence.

"A storm is coming."

6

"What's that supposed to mean?"

In the sickly glare of the flashlight beam, Johnny's expression looks angry and strange, the shadows falling across his face in all the wrong places.

"I don't know," I say, the same question running through my brain. "I'm not the one who sent the message."

Sweat drips from my face onto the open page of the exercise book, smudging the letters I've marked there. The air feels almost thick enough to touch, the sweltering heat of the day still trapped beneath the roof of leaves even though night has fallen. I reach up to wipe my face with my hand, the bandage now sticky against my forehead.

"A storm is coming." Dizzy repeats the words softly, almost under his breath, as if weighing the truth in them. "You don't want to be in the woods in a storm."

"Why not?" I say, almost wishing that a storm would come to puncture this heat. "The trees will keep us dry."

"It's not the rain you need to worry about in a storm," Dizzy replies. "It's the lightning."

He sweeps his flashlight around so it's aiming at the tree that lies fallen behind us. The stumps of its broken branches cast eerie shadows as the yellow beam plays across the deadwood, but then on its underside I see a dark scar running the length of the trunk. It looks like the bark has been torn from the tree there, exposing charred wood underneath.

"Lightning always strikes the highest point," Dizzy says. "And in a wood that's always a tree."

I suddenly realize that this blackened crack is a lightning scar. That must be what brought the tree down.

"*Beware the oak; it draws the stroke,*" Johnny says, his words coming out in a singsong fashion. "*Avoid an ash; it courts the flash.*" Shadows flash across his leering face as Dizzy swings the flashlight round again. "Everyone knows that, especially birds."

Frowning, I close the exercise book, stuffing it and the pencil back into Dizzy's bag as I clamber to my feet. I didn't know that. They didn't teach us stupid songs about the countryside at my school in London. Away from the flashlight beam's dazzling glare, the woods seem even darker than before. I wish I were back there now. It's never this dark in London.

"So we need to get out of here," I say, holding out my hand for Dizzy's flashlight. "Can I borrow that?"

Reluctantly Dizzy hands the flashlight over. Its metal case feels slick to the touch, but the weight of it in my hand makes me feel just a tiny bit better. With this, I can keep the dark at bay.

I sweep the flashlight around in a circle, trying to work out which way to go. Its fuzzy beam illuminates the trees, sculpting them into leafy statues. Beneath their tangled limbs, several narrow tracks head off in different directions, each one trailing into the same inky dimness.

"So which way do we go?" Johnny says.

I don't know.

The flashlight beam wavers as I try to trace each trail through the trees, trying to decide which track to choose. I can see the broken branch where Johnny pushed his way out of the trees. No chance of finding the path that way if what he said is true. And no point in climbing over the lightning-scarred trunk to head back the way we came.

I hold the flashlight steady, its yellow light falling along a narrow track that lies halfway between the two. This crooked trail looks the same as all the others, wildflowers and ferns sprouting in the leaf litter as it winds between the trees. Perhaps it's my imagination, but the flashlight beam seems to shine a little brighter here. Maybe that's a sign.

"This way," I say, trying to make my voice sound more certain than I am. "Follow me."

Striding forward, I start to make my way along the trail. Behind me, I hear Dizzy and Johnny hurrying to catch up.

"Wait for us!"

The track is so narrow we have to walk in single file, the spaces between the trees completely shut in by the surrounding undergrowth. I can hear faint rustling sounds, the tread of tiny unseen creatures scurrying for cover as we pass. I keep my eyes fixed on the yellow beam of light as it splashes along the track, illuminating the exposed tree roots lying in wait to trip me. I step over them, brushing past an overhanging branch that reaches out to bar the way.

"Watch out!" Dizzy shouts as the branch snaps back behind me.

"Sorry," I call back, but there's not much I can do as I have to push my way past another low branch, its bark rough against my fingers.

In the light thrown by the flashlight the trees look reassuringly solid, but away from it they melt again into shadow. Dead sticks snap beneath my feet, making my heart skip a beat. I can't help feeling as if someone's watching me—just out of sight in the trees. I keep my eyes fixed to the ground, so easy now to stumble and fall.

In the distance I hear a sudden bark and freeze, gripping the flashlight tightly.

"Is that a dog?" I say, turning round to find Dizzy right behind me. "Maybe someone is out looking for us?"

Screwing up his eyes, Dizzy flinches as the flashlight shines in his face.

"Sorry," I say, quickly lowering the beam.

The bark comes again, farther away this time.

Blinking, Dizzy shakes his head.

"No," he says. "That's a fox."

Dizzy's reply snuffs out the flicker of hope that sparked inside my chest. There's no search party out there. Nobody even knows where we are.

I grip the flashlight more tightly as I turn to push on again. All we can do is keep following this track. Above my head the twisting branches are close enough to touch, making me feel as though I'm tunneling through the woods. As I walk, the wavering flashlight beam drives the darkness back foot by foot. I only hope that I'll find light at the end of this tunnel.

"What makes you think this is the right way?" Johnny calls out as the track begins to twist.

I don't know, so I pretend I haven't heard him.

As I duck beneath another low branch, the track begins to narrow again as it turns left and then sharply right. I feel as though I'm being squeezed as the trees crowd ever closer. Then the path turns sharply left again and suddenly opens into a small clearing.

"What is it?"

"Have you found the path?"

Dizzy and Johnny's questions trail into silence as they join me in the clearing. I sweep the flashlight beam round the circle of trees, the bushes and thickets between them forming an impenetrable wall. There's no way forward. There's no way out. It's a dead end.

"I thought you said this was the right way!" Johnny explodes, his anger as hot as the sweltering air.

I take a step back, the glow of the flashlight catching a glimmer of white on the ground.

"What's that?"

Stepping forward, I aim the flashlight beam down, Dizzy and Johnny crowding round to see what I've found.

There are dozens of sticks laid out on the ground. Some are pointing like arrows in different directions, others set at right angles or arranged into squares. But every single stick is smooth and white, the bark stripped off each one.

I look up at Johnny, a fresh surge of anger rising in my chest.

"You left these here," I say, the flashlight in my hand shaking as I fight the urge to hit Johnny with it. "You're trying to trick us again."

But Johnny's face is deathly pale as he stares down at the sticks on the ground.

"I didn't," he says, his voice barely louder than a whisper. "I wouldn't dare. I swear. This stuff is secret."

"What do you mean 'secret'?" I ask, reluctant to believe a word that Johnny says.

Johnny shakes his head.

"I can't tell you. My dad would murder me if I did."

"What's your dad got to do with this?" I glance down again at the sticks on the ground, noticing for the first time the smooth white pebbles between some of them. "Your dad's a butcher—not some spy leaving secret messages."

Dizzy crouches next to the sticks, his notebook open again as he starts to sketch the symbols. But before he's even finished the first line, Johnny snatches the book out of his hand.

"Hey!"

"My dad's not just a butcher," Johnny growls, ripping the page from the book and screwing it up in his fist. "He's a Freemason, and this stuff is secret."

Beneath the sweat-soaked bandage, my head aches. I'm so mad at Johnny now. All I want to do is find the way home, but he's more bothered about keeping secrets.

"It's the only clue we've got," I say, keeping the flashlight trained on the strange symbols on the ground. "We're lost in the woods, and this might help us to find a way out. If you know what it means then you've got to tell us."

Still holding his pencil in his hand, Dizzy climbs to his feet. The three of us stand in the small circle of light that's reflecting off the ground, but beyond that the darkness surrounds us.

"Please, Johnny." Dizzy's voice cuts through the gloom. "I just want to get home. Don't you?"

Johnny looks from Dizzy to me and then back again. The shadows cast across his face fall upward, almost making it look as if I can see the skull beneath his skin.

"OK," he says, reaching out to take the pencil from Dizzy, "but if you tell *anyone* that I showed you this, I'll kill you."

1

"This is the Freemasons' code," Johnny says, resting the open book on his knee as we all crouch to inspect the strange symbols laid out on the ground.

In the beam of the flashlight, the sticks and pebbles shine bone-white against the golden-green leaves.

"Aren't the Freemasons some kind of secret society?" I say, remembering what I've read about them in one of my dad's Sherlock Holmes stories.

Johnny nods solemnly.

"All the important people in our village are Freemasons," he says, keeping his voice low, as if he's afraid of being overheard. "Dr. Hazell, Sergeant Burrows, even Twiggy, our headmaster."

The shadows are edging closer, but I can't stop myself from smiling at the thought of Mr. Twigg belonging to a secret society. He's never mentioned it in assembly.

"My dad's in charge of them all," Johnny continues, his dark eyes gleaming in the flashlight's glare. "He's the Master of the Lodge and keeps all the Freemasons' secrets written down in this code."

I glance down at the symbols on the ground.

"Tell us what this says, then."

Johnny hesitates for a second, the pencil twitching nervously between his fingers, before he starts to sketch out a grid on the page. It looks like he's getting ready for a game of tic-tac-toe, but then he draws the same grid again, this time placing a dot in each square. Beneath these grids he draws two crosses, adding more dots to the second again.

"In the Freemasons' code, each letter of the alphabet is shown by the part of the grid that it's found in," Johnny says, filling in each of the blank spaces he's made with a different letter until the alphabet is complete.

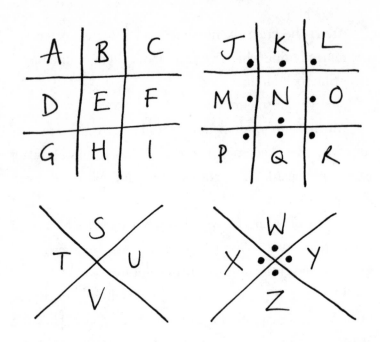

Looking up from the page, Johnny points at the first symbol on the ground: two sticks laid out in the shape of an arrowhead.

"This is the letter 'T,'" he explains, holding up the book and tapping the page where the symbol can be found.

"So what do the rest say?" Dizzy asks.

I hold the flashlight steady as my eyes quickly flick between the bone-white sticks and the grids that Johnny's drawn, decoding the symbols letter by letter as Johnny scribbles them down on the page.

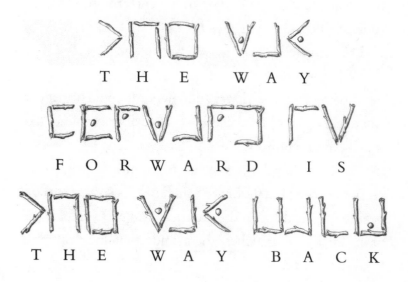

T H E   W A Y

F O R W A R D   I S

T H E   W A Y   B A C K

We reach the end of the line at exactly the same time, both of us speaking the message out loud.

"The way forward is the way back."

Instinctively, we cross our fingers to ward off the jinx of saying the same words at the same time. But then, from the darkness that surrounds us, comes the sound of laughter.

We jump as one, a prickle of fear spiking my skin as I swing the flashlight around the clearing. The seesawing beam illuminates the bushes and trees, the dense thicket looking even thicker than it did before. No way in or out, except the way we came.

"Who's there?" I call out.

The high-pitched laughter fades into silence, the darkness hiding its secrets once more. Beneath my bandage I can hear the blood pounding in my ears, the sound like a thunderstorm inside my head.

I turn toward Dizzy; his face is frozen in fear.

"What was that?"

"I—I don't know," Dizzy stammers. "It could be a green woodpecker, maybe. Sometimes its call can sound like somebody laughing."

The manic laugh rings out again, coming from every direction. I swing the flashlight round like a sword, its yellow beam scything through the darkness. But all I see is a maze of impenetrable branches, the sound of madness dripping from their leaves.

Johnny swears.

"That's not a bird," he says, his fists clenched, ready to clobber anything that moves out of the trees. "Don't you see—it's the person who left this message for us. They're laughing because they've got us trapped in this dead end."

I glance down at the symbols on the ground, the sticks scattered by our panic when we leapt to our feet. In the ghostly glare of the flashlight they almost look like bones. With a sickening lurch, I realize who the laugh belongs to.

Ha—ha—ha—ha . . .

Old Crony.

"Come on!" Johnny shouts into the darkness as the laughing call comes again. "Show yourself!"

I shake my head in fear. Please don't.

The raving laughter is getting louder now, each cackle accompanied by a crack, like a branch being torn from a tree. As quickly as I swing the flashlight round in the direction of each sound, I catch only glimpses of shadows in the trees.

"I don't like this," Dizzy says, grabbing his notebook from the ground and stuffing it into his school bag. "We've got to get out of here."

The sound of another laugh right behind me makes me spin round. In the flashlight's flailing beam I glimpse the dark shape of a figure fading into the trees.

"It's over there!"

But as Dizzy and Johnny turn to look, only the imprint of the dark remains, and all we can see is the twisting track leading through the trees.

The way forward is the way back.

Snatching the flashlight from my hand, Johnny heads in the direction of the track as the laughter rings out again.

"Follow me!"

Dizzy does what he's told, hurrying to catch Johnny as the flashlight beam lights up the trail. For a second, I stand there, frozen to the spot as the darkness grows around me.

Then I hear a gentle laugh and a single word whispered in my ear.

"Charlie."

I run.

8

I don't know how long I keep running, following the flickering flashlight beam as it cuts through the trees. Long enough for a stitch to start burning in my side. Long enough for the track to turn to mud beneath my feet. Long enough to leave the sound of laughter behind, but not the memory of the voice whispering my name.

"Charlie!"

The flashlight beam swings back in my direction. I stagger to a halt, my breath coming in juddering gasps as Johnny and Dizzy loom out of the gloom. Pushing past me, Johnny aims the flashlight back the way we came.

"Has it followed us?"

I turn to look, my heart still pounding in my chest at the thought of Old Crony on our trail. But when I look back all I can see are the trees. It's as if the track was never there, the yellow glow of the flashlight illuminating only a maze of tangled branches.

"This can't be right," Johnny says, shaking his head in confusion. "Where's the track gone?"

I don't know the answer. I look around, searching the darkness for any kind of clue. There are no paths to choose, just a solid rise of tree trunks that cut across any kind of view.

"How are we going to get out of here?" Dizzy asks, his voice almost despairing.

The flashlight flickers, its yellow beam fading slightly as the darkness creeps closer.

I just want to go home.

If I close my eyes I can almost imagine I'm there, curled up in bed with a book in my hand. But then against my skin I feel the cold breeze that's blowing through the trees, the rustling leaves sounding like a single word being endlessly repeated.

Lost . . . Lost . . . Lost . . .

My eyes snap open as I realize what we've got to do.

In *Scouting for Boys* there's a whole section on what you need to know if you ever get lost when out on patrol. Most of it is completely useless now, as there's no point looking for landmarks when all we can see are trees. But there's one way we can find our way in the dark.

"We can use the stars to guide us," I say, the words

rushing out in my excitement. "All we need to do is find the North Star and then we can follow this out of the wood."

"How can we follow a star?" Johnny asks. "This isn't the Nativity."

"The North Star is called the North Star because it lies directly above the North Pole," I say, remembering the explanation from Dad's scouting book. "All the other stars move around the sky during the night, but the North Star always stays in the same place. If you walk directly toward it—wherever you are—you know you'll be heading true north. That's how we can find our way out of the woods. Just keep heading north until we hit the road that skirts the top of the wood, and then we can follow this back to the village."

Hope rising, we all look up at the same time to see a pitch-black sky. It takes a second or two for my eyes to adjust away from the glare of the flashlight, but then I realize it isn't that the sky is black but that the woods themselves have shut out the sky. The crisscrossing branches hold up a roof of leaves, now painted the color of night.

"So much for your bright idea," Johnny sneers. "We can't even see the stars."

Frustrated, I rest my hand against the low bough of a nearby tree, drumming my fingers against it. I thought I'd found a way to escape, but the trees seem to hide every way out.

The feel of the rough bark beneath my fingers seems

suddenly familiar to me. The memory of another time and place travels from the tips of my fingers until a forgotten moment flowers again in my mind. I remember a picnic in the park, sitting squashed between my parents on a blanket beneath a tree. I remember staring up into its branches, telling Mum and Dad that I reckoned I could climb all the way to the top. Then I remember my dad suddenly lifting me up, his hands around my waist as he hoisted me into the branches. "Go on, then," he said, the look on his face challenging me to prove that I wasn't a disappointment. I remember starting to climb, my toes squeezing into the grooves in the bark as my fingers scrabbled for the next handhold. I remember clambering higher and higher until the branches started to bend beneath my touch. Then I remember looking down at my parents' upturned faces, so much smaller than I thought they'd be, my heart bursting with pride and terror as I clung to the crown of the tree.

The memory makes my heart ache as I stare up into the shadowy branches. But it also shows me how we can find our way home.

"If we climb above the leaves, we'll be able to see the stars," I say. "If we get high enough, we might even be able to see the lights from the village and then we'll know exactly which way to go."

Slinging his bag to the ground, Dizzy slumps against the trunk of the tree that I'm leaning against.

"I'm not exactly cut out for climbing trees, Charlie," he

says quietly, stretching out his bad leg as he sits with his back to the tree.

"I—I didn't mean you," I stutter, the shadows falling across Dizzy's face unable to hide his grimace as he rubs his right knee. "Johnny's the tallest—he should be the one to climb up."

"No way," says Johnny, swinging the flashlight so it's aiming straight up into the branches. "That tree's at least a hundred feet tall. I'd break my neck if I tried to climb it in the dark."

I tilt my head upward as the yellow glare of the flashlight illuminates the boughs and branches rising from the vast trunk. Between their leaves I glimpse green acorn cups, the oak's sturdy branches turning into walkways in my mind as my gaze climbs the tree. The flashlight beam turns to mist before it reaches the highest branches, unable to show a way through their curtain of leaves, but the feel of the rough bark beneath my fingers tells me I could get to the top.

"I could climb it," I say, turning toward Johnny. "If you're scared of heights."

Lowering the flashlight, Johnny fixes me with a scornful stare.

"Don't be stupid, Charlotte," he says, using the name that he knows I hate. "Girls can't climb trees."

I feel myself bristle. I'm not stupid, and I'm sick of people telling me what I can or can't do. Whether it's my dad telling me I can't join the scouts or Johnny saying girls can't climb trees. I can do anything a boy can do. Reaching down, I take off my shoes and socks, and then, before Dizzy can even start to protest, I catch hold of the lowest bough and hoist myself up.

"Charlie!" Dizzy scrambles to his feet. "What are you doing?"

"Climbing the tree," I say, my bare feet gripping the grooves in the bark as I reach forward toward the trunk. "Keep that flashlight pointing up to give me some light."

Using the trunk as a banister, I lever myself up on to the next branch. Twisting upward to the left and right are more branches, and testing my weight on each of these in turn, I start to work my way up the tree, my anger helping me to haul myself higher. Twigs and leaves brush against my face as I climb; then I spit as a furry caterpillar lands upon my lips, my body swaying as I bring up my free hand to quickly wipe it away.

It's getting darker, the leaves spreading out beneath me now hiding the flashlight's beam. I brace myself against the trunk, trusting my hands and feet to find the safest holds. I feel like I'm escaping into another dimension, my fingers tingling as a fresh breeze rustles the leaves around me.

According to Miss James, we come from the trees. Human beings, that is. In class the other day she was telling us about Charles Darwin and his theory of evolution. She said that scientists now think that our oldest ancestors were apes who lived their whole lives in the trees. Maybe that's what's helping me climb—I'm just remembering how we used to live.

My hands feel clammy as I haul myself higher, the branches around me starting to thin. As I reach for the next one I hear Johnny shout from far below, the sound making me glance down in surprise.

"Can you see anything yet?"

Then my hand closes around empty air, my body swinging sideways as the branch I was reaching for turns out to be a mirage. Darkness yawns beneath me as my feet begin to slip, but then my fingers find the furrowed bark of the trunk and I grab hold with every ounce of strength I have left.

"Charlie!" Dizzy's voice sounds like it's coming from miles away. "Are you OK?"

I can't even open my mouth to reply as I cling to the tree for dear life. I screw my eyes shut, pressing my face against the rough bark as the world spins around me.

As my ear flattens against the tree trunk, I feel a strange vibration pulsing through it. At first I think it must be the blood pumping through my veins, my heart still hammering in my chest. But then I realize that the rhythm I can feel isn't a pulse, but a melody.

And that's when I hear the music coming from the heart of the tree.

9

It's the same dance music that Dad always plays on a Friday night, the sound drifting up the stairs to my room. The swelling melody makes me feel sick as I cling to the swaying trunk, my eyes still screwed tightly shut. I hear the staccato horns as they punch out the rhythm of the song, the beat winding its way from deep inside the tree straight into my ear.

I hold my breath, trying to make sense of it. People say that when you hold a shell to your ear you can sometimes hear the sound of the sea. But as the rough bark scratches my face, all I can hear now is the sound of music. My mind reels, the world spinning as the song flows through me.

Then I hear my dad's voice suddenly loud above the music.

"No! You listen to me!"

My fingers slip, the sound of Dad's voice almost jolting me out of the tree. When I'm up in my room this is usually the signal for me to clamp my hands over my ears, desperate to block out the sound of the argument that I know is on the way. But I can't do that now.

Instead I cling grimly to the tree, feeling the bark splinter beneath my fingernails as my parents' voices rage within. I can't hear what they're arguing about—only the odd angry word punctuated by the sound of a plate smashing against the wall. Dad said that things would be better when we moved here, but the arguments have been getting worse.

Mum and Dad arguing about all the things that have gone wrong.

Mum and Dad arguing about how to put them right.

Arguing about the future.

Arguing about the past.

Arguing about me.

And there's nothing I can do to make them stop.

I want to shout at them. Tell them that I'm lost in the woods and that I need them to come and find me. But as their argument storms, my words only come out in a whisper, my whole body shaking as a fresh gust of wind rocks the tree.

"Help me."

Then the music swells, drowning out Mum and Dad's

screaming voices. For a second, it's all I can hear before the tree suddenly shudders with the sound of a door slamming shut. The song is cut off into silence and all I can hear now is the rustling of leaves.

Even though my eyes are still closed, I can feel the tears rolling down my face.

Then I hear the sound of Dizzy's voice, calling from the ground below.

"Charlie!"

I force my eyes open, unable even to reach up to wipe the tears away. My hands grip the tree trunk, the pain I can feel seeping into its fissures as the darkness surrounds me.

"Charlie!" Dizzy calls out again. "Are you OK? What can you see?"

Tilting my head, I peer up into the inky blackness, my eyes slowly adjusting to the dark. Through the thinning branches, I can see slivers of silvery light splashing through the leaves.

"I'm nearly there," I call out, the words tasting like dust in my bone-dry mouth.

Gritting my teeth, I reach up to the slender branch above my head, praying it won't break as I haul myself higher. My arm aches, fear thumping in my chest as the tree sways again. But then my head breaks through this final curtain of leaves and I'm forced to squint as a sudden brightness fills my eyes.

Blinking, I look up to see the moon shining down directly

overhead. It looks almost close enough to touch—if I dared to let go of the tree—a swollen crescent, white against the darkness of the sky. My head spins as I take a deep breath, the air sharp and cold up here.

My eyes scan the horizon as I try to get my bearings.

I'm searching for a sight of the village, certain that I'll be able to glimpse its lights somewhere in the distance, but all I can see is a dark-green carpet of leaves, the moonlight illuminating the tops of the trees. Holding tight to the branch, I crane my neck in the opposite direction, but my gaze just rolls along an unbroken sea of treetops. The woods stretch out in every direction as far as my eyes can see.

In the distance, I hear the *chk-chk* sound of a nightjar and I remember with a shiver its Morse-code call.

A storm is coming.

Fighting to keep my fear under control, I lift my head to the sky. The lie of the land might be making it look like the trees go on forever, but if I can find the North Star we'll still be able to find our way out of the woods.

According to *Scouting for Boys*, the best way to find the North Star is to look for the Plough, a group of seven bright stars that, when you draw lines between them, make the shape of a plough in the sky. Although I think they look more like a saucepan. The two stars at the tip of the Plough are called the Pointers because these point the way to where the North Star is.

I blink, my eyes taking a moment again to adjust to the full glare of the moonlight. From up here the stars seem so much brighter than I've ever seen them before. But as I search the sky for the familiar shape of the Plough, I realize that something's wrong.

It's not just the brightness of the stars that hurts my eyes, but the patterns they make in the sky. I can't see the Plough pointing the way to the North Star. The stars look all wrong. I stare up in confusion, trying to make sense of the pinpricks of light scattered across the darkness.

There's no sign of Orion or any of the other constellations that the scouting book said I should learn to find my way in the dark. For a second I think that I've found Cassiopeia, but then I realize that the final two stars look all wrong: the familiar W-shape of the constellation flattened into a question mark.

This isn't right. The constellations should always look the same no matter where they are in the sky. I used to stare out my bedroom window at night, memorizing their shapes and wishing I could just float off among them to escape. But now their strangeness scares me.

"Charlie!" The sound of Dizzy's voice pulls my head out of the stars. "Are you all right up there?"

I shake my head, my fingers trembling as I cling to the tree. I thought by climbing up here I'd find the way out, but I feel more lost now than I ever did before.

"I'm coming down."

As the roof of leaves closes over my head, it's almost a relief to descend into the darkness again, the leaves whipping back against my face as I clamber from one branch to the next.

I have to look down with every step I take, making sure that each foothold I find won't send me tumbling out of the tree. My heart thuds in my chest, the fear so much worse than when I climbed up. Between the branches I catch glimpses of the ground far below, the tiny figures of Dizzy and Johnny almost lost among the shadows.

Down and down and down I go, the moments blurring into an endless nightmare as I descend. But then I'm pushing past the last curtain of leaves, the yellow glare of the flashlight beam swinging up to greet me as my feet touch down on the final bough.

"Charlie!"

Dizzy scrambles to help me down from the tree, my body shaking uncontrollably as I finally feel the earth between my toes.

"Are you all right?"

I feel Dizzy's arm on my shoulder, his voice filled with concern, but as I look up the first face I see is Johnny's looking down at me.

"So," he says, "did you see which way we have to go?"

I look around. Beyond the fuzzy circle of light cast by the flashlight, the woods seem even darker than before. The spaces between the trees are painted black, and as I peer into their shadows I can't stop myself from picturing the strange constellations that filled the night sky. No sign of the North Star. No way of knowing which way to go.

Looking up to meet Johnny's gaze, there's only one thing I can say.

"No."

There's no way out.

10

"I told you girls can't climb trees," Johnny explodes. "We've wasted all this time waiting for you when we could have been finding our way out of here."

I pull on my socks and shoes as Johnny waves the flashlight wildly around the trees.

"Tell the truth, *Charlotte*. You just got stuck on one of the bottom branches and were too embarrassed to come down."

I feel my face flush with anger as I climb slowly to my feet. Next to me, Dizzy holds out a hand to help me up, but I brush it away. My body aches, but I don't need any help. I made it to the top of the tree. I just don't know how to explain what I saw there.

"What's the point in finding the North Star anyway?" Johnny continues, swinging the flashlight round in a circle. Its fuzzy beam illuminates the broad trunks of the trees and the bushes that lie between them. "All we need to do is pick one direction and then stick to it. We're bound to find our way out eventually. The woods can't go on forever."

I remember what I saw as I clung to the swaying tree-top, the moonlight illuminating an unbroken sea of leaves. I take a deep breath, ready to tell Johnny that it looked to me as if the woods covered the whole world.

But then I hear voices in the distance.

The sound is so faint that at first I think I'm mistaken, but then the murmuring noise comes again, drifting through the trees away to the right.

"Did you hear that?" I ask, keeping my voice low in case I drown out the sound.

"Yes," Dizzy breathes as he peers into the darkness. "Maybe someone's come to find us."

Thoughts of Mum and Dad swim into my mind. We've been gone for hours now. The first thing they would've done when I didn't come home on time is march round to Dizzy's house. And then when they found out I wasn't there, maybe the woods is where they'd look next. Maybe they're all looking for us. Mum. Dad. Dizzy's parents. Maybe even Johnny's dad.

"We're over here!" Johnny shouts, waving his flashlight in the direction of the sound.

But then I remember the sound of the voice whispering in my ear. *Charlie.*

"Shush," I say, holding up my hand to try to stop Johnny from shouting out again. "He might hear us."

"What do you mean?" Johnny says, flashing me a contemptuous stare. "We want them to hear us. Don't you realize—they're looking for us."

He turns away, holding the flashlight high as he aims it into the trees.

"We're over here!" he calls, walking toward the sound. "Follow the sound of my voice."

I glance across at Dizzy, a strange expression of hope and fear on his face as the darkness sweeps over us. Johnny is already disappearing into the trees, the yellow glow of the flashlight quickly fading as he calls out again.

"This way!"

We don't have any choice if we don't want to be left in the dark.

Hurrying to catch up, we follow Johnny.

He's only a short way ahead, pushing through a curtain of ferns. Shadows dance between their leaves, and I hold my breath as a low babble of voices rises in the distance. As my heart quickens, I feel Dizzy's hand steal into mine as he gives it a reassuring squeeze.

"Over here!" he shouts, his voice echoing Johnny's as they both call out again. "We're over here!"

I pull my hand free to push past the ferns, Dizzy following close behind as we find Johnny waiting for us in a circle of light. He holds out a hand to tell us to keep quiet.

The three of us stand completely still, ears straining against the dark as we wait for an answering call from the search party that must be out there.

"Over *here!*" Johnny shouts, flicking the flashlight on and off to signal where we are.

But in the darkness between each flash, a worrying thought creeps into my head: What if they're not coming to find us? What if they're coming to get us instead?

"Who's out there?" I say, keeping my voice low as the distant voices seem to blend into one. But inside my head I can't stop myself from answering my own question.

Old Crony.

I turn toward Dizzy. A frown furrows my friend's face as he strains to make out the sound. Then his concentration suddenly breaks as his eyes open wide.

"This isn't voices we hear," he says, reaching out to grab the flashlight from Johnny's hand. "It's running water."

As Dizzy's words sink in, the murmuring sound seems to shift in my mind. Instead of a babble of voices, I can now make out the burbling sound of water rushing over stone.

It isn't Old Crony. There's no search party coming to find us.

"Great!" Johnny spits out the word. "So we're still lost."

"No, you don't understand," Dizzy says, a fresh note of hope in his voice. "There's a river that runs through the woods. If we've found that, then all we need to do is follow it to find our way out."

With the flashlight in his hand, Dizzy beckons for us to follow him. The beam seems much fainter than before as we push on through the trees, illuminating only a few paces ahead.

The darkness seems to play tricks as we search for the river. Sometimes the babbling seems to be coming from the right, but then, as we turn in that direction, the sound shifts and we hear splashing instead from the left. It's as though we're lost in a wild labyrinth, stumbling over roots and dead branches as we follow the thread of the sound between the trees.

Beneath my feet sprays of white flowers and green leaves disguise the muddy ground. A wild garlicky smell fills the darkness, reminding me in a rush of the time Dad took us to a fancy restaurant in London for a birthday treat. It was called Gennaro's, and we all had to wear our very best clothes. I remember Mum blushing when the waiter gave her a flower at the door, Dad frowning slightly as he bustled us to our seats and then this same garlicky smell wafting through the kitchen doors as the waiters barged them open.

We were happy then, I think.

Up ahead the trees are starting to thin, a faint silvery light splashing through their branches as the ground begins to slope.

"We've found it!" Johnny shouts, his voice ringing out in triumph.

He starts to scramble down the leafy bank with Dizzy close behind. Beyond them, I can see the river, drenched in moonlight as it winds its way through the trees. The sound of soft murmuring voices surrounds us as the rushing water flows.

Johnny is already striding ahead, toward a wooden bridge that spans the river. I don't know why he's bothering. The water looks so shallow you could walk across it without getting your ankles wet.

Slithering down the bank, I join Dizzy by the water's edge. He reaches to pick up a stone that's lying on the ground. He holds it in his hand, the moonlight illuminating the strange grooves and veins that mark its surface.

"What's that?" I ask.

"Brainstone," Dizzy replies. "That's what some people call it, anyway. You find it here sometimes along the riverbank."

He hands me the stone, the feel of it cold and smooth against my skin. Its marbled surface is marked with dark bands and speckled ridges between lighter bands of white and gray. In the pale light the patterns look like a forest of trees set against a brightening sky, almost as if the woods themselves are etched onto the stone.

"Hundreds of millions of years ago, all of this was under the sea," Dizzy says, sweeping the flashlight across the shallow river until its sickly beam lights up the trees on the opposite side. "These woods would have been the shore of an ancient ocean—mudflats stretching for miles until they reached the sea."

Peering down again at the stone, Dizzy points at the speckled bands as I cradle it in my hand.

"This limestone was made when the tiny worms that lived in these mudflats grew upward in search of the sun. That's what these dark bits are made of—*worms*. The lighter bits are where mud got trapped in the hollows in between. And over time all these different layers were pushed together until they finally made this limestone."

I stare at my friend in astonishment. When Miss James asks us questions in class, Dizzy never says a word, but listening to him now, it's like he knows everything.

Dizzy turns away, his flashlight playing across the stones scattered at the river's edge.

"That's what a lot of these stones are," he says. "Fossils of the very first things that ever lived."

Fascinated, I turn the stone over in my hands. As I trace its patterns and ridges with my fingers, I realize why Dizzy called it brainstone. In a science book at school there's a picture of a human brain. That's what this stone looks like—a broken chunk of brain.

I think it's funny that people all look so different on the outside, but inside our heads, our brains all look the same.

I can't help thinking it should be the other way round, as it's the thoughts inside our heads that make us unique.

I reach up to touch the bandage that's wrapped around my head, wanting to make sure my own brain hasn't started leaking out, but it's bone-dry. My head's even stopped aching now.

Then I feel a wetness in the hollow of my other hand. I glance down, and my mouth falls open in astonishment as I watch the stone I'm holding start to melt into mud. I can feel tiny worms squirming between my fingers, the once-solid rock now turned into a scoop of living mud. My head spins as I take a sharp breath, the warm air salty on my tongue.

"Charlie?"

Dizzy's voice seems to be coming from a distance as the mud slowly drips through my fingers.

"Charlie!"

I feel a hand on my shoulder, and my head snaps up.

"Are you OK?" Dizzy asks, slowly pulling his hand away as he peers at me in concern.

I look down again and see the stone resting in the hollow of my hand. My fingers are dry, showing no trace of the mud I felt seeping through them only moments ago. The stone looks exactly the same as it did before. The same as it's looked for millions of years. Solid. Unchanged.

I shake my head. I think I'm going mad.

"Are you OK?" Dizzy asks again, a real note of worry in his voice.

I let the stone fall from my fingers and hear it hit the ground with a clack.

"I'm fine," I say, looking up to peer along the riverbank. "Let's go."

Dizzy hikes his schoolbag higher on his shoulder.

"If we follow the river this way," he says, "then we should be heading west. Eventually it should bring us out on to Chase Lane, and we can follow that back to the village."

Up ahead I see Johnny start to cross the wooden bridge that spans the river, his figure silhouetted in the silvery moonlight. As he reaches the center, he turns to glance in our direction.

"Come on!"

His voice cuts through the night. In front of the bridge, I can see the brightness of the moon reflected in the water, dazzling against the darkness.

I look up and see the moon is full.

I blink.

It wasn't before.

Then I hear Johnny shout, the sound quickly followed by a splash.

I look down to see that the bridge has disappeared into mist, and I catch a glimpse of Johnny's arm before it vanishes beneath the surface of the water.

11

I move without thinking, tearing off my shoes and socks before I launch myself into the river.

I'm expecting to be able to wade through the water toward the place where I saw Johnny fall, but instead find myself gasping in shock as I plunge in waist-deep. The stones beneath my feet slip away as the riverbed swiftly shelves and I'm forced to kick, my arms stretching out in a breaststroke, just to keep my head above the surface of the water.

Feeling confused, I glance back over my shoulder to see what's happening, but I can't see the riverbank. Dizzy and even the woods themselves are now lost in a mist that seems to rise from the water. I look toward the sky, desperately treading water to keep myself afloat, but even the moon is hidden behind the shroud of mist. All I can see is the swell of the water surrounding me, each white-tipped wave rising higher than the last.

This doesn't feel like a river anymore. I feel like I'm lost at sea.

Then, out there in the darkness, I hear Johnny's voice. "Charlie!"

I kick out in the direction of the sound. The swell momentarily lifts me as I swim into an oncoming wave; then I feel myself dropped as its spray crashes over my head. The water is so cold, the taste of salt on my lips making no sense at all. With every stroke I take, I feel the waves pushing me back, and it's all I can do to claw through the surging foam.

Panic starts to bubble in my chest, my heart racing as I snatch another breath. I thought I'd be able to drag Johnny out of the river, but as the waves chop into me I don't know if I'll even be able to save myself. A creeping sense of dread invades my head, and I can't stop myself from glancing down into the water. Beneath the spray, I can't see the riverbed, just an inky blackness that seems to stretch fathoms deep. Where am I?

I grit my teeth to stop them from chattering, the rising fear numbing my senses as I search in vain for a way out. But then, between the waves, I catch a glimpse of Johnny, his head bobbing above the water like a cork.

I strike out toward him, my arms and legs thrashing through the water, until I finally reach his side.

Johnny's head is tilted back, his mouth barely above the surface. As his eyes lock on mine, his flailing arms reach toward me, and I have to push him away to stop him from dragging me under.

"Stop panicking," I say, desperately treading water as the waves swell around us.

"Can't swim," Johnny gasps, his eyes wide with terror. "Legs—stuck."

He swallows another gulp of water, and I realize that he's drowning in front of my eyes.

"Help me."

There's only one thing I can do. Taking a deep breath, I duck my head beneath the foaming surface, peeling back the water with my hands as I angle my body downward, then kick as I dive to find out what's trapping Johnny. The freezing-cold water is churned into confusion, and it takes me a second to work out what I'm seeing.

Legs kick out amid a tangle of netting, twisting ropes snaring Johnny like a fish. But as I swim down to try to free him, I realize with a sudden lurch of fear that this can't be Johnny. Bubbles of air escape from my lips as I blink in blank confusion at the thrashing figure. This isn't a boy, but a man.

He's dressed in a browny-green uniform, the brass

buttons on the front of his jacket shining amid the water's murk. I can't see the man's face, as his head is tilted back above the surface, but as I look down at the netting that's tangled round his brown leather boots, I know that if I can't free him, he'll drown.

Somewhere above my head, I hear muffled groans and howls, followed by a distant boom that thuds through the water. It sounds as if the world is falling apart. But I can't do anything about that now. My heart hammers in my throat as I try to pull the man's feet free from the twisted net. I'm running out of air, the roaring inside my head getting louder every second.

My numbed fingers scrabble uselessly against the fraying ropes as they twist and twine, the muffled sound of a tolling bell now ringing through the water. As I hear this, fragments of thoughts swim into my mind. I see myself standing in front of the village church, staring up at the bell tower with a strange sense of dread as the rain soaks me through. Then I'm lining up outside my class as the school bell rings, watching Johnny aim a sly flick at Dizzy's ear as Miss James walks on by. Then the swell of the crowd sweeps me off my feet, everybody cheering in celebration as Big Ben chimes midnight. Forgotten memories merge into imagined moments, each one jostling for attention as the bell tolls. Light bleeds into my brain, the weight of the water slowly disappearing as I start to let go.

Then another boom stirs the water around me, and I feel the netting shift beneath my fingers. With one last desperate tug, I manage to pry it off the man's boots, and watch as his legs float free. Then I kick for the surface with every ounce of strength I have left, breaking through the waves with a breathless gasp.

I look around and catch sight of Johnny spluttering as he lifts his head clear of the waves. Their white-tipped crests rise and fall around us, revealing nothing more.

The man is gone.

"Charlie!"

From somewhere to my left comes the sound of Dizzy's voice. Hearing this, I strike out in the direction of the sound, glancing back as I snatch a breath to check that Johnny's following me. My whole body aches, and as the currents drag us forward, I can't help fearing that every tiring stroke is going to be my last.

"This way!"

We swim toward Dizzy's voice, the mists that cling to the tops of the waves slowly clearing before we glimpse Dizzy at the water's edge. And then I feel the stones beneath my feet and stumble forward through the shallows until Dizzy hauls me out onto the riverbank.

Water drips onto my face as Johnny collapses by my side. We lie there for what feels like forever, unable to speak as our breath comes in ragged gasps. When my heart finally slows to what still feels like double speed, I manage to pull myself to a seated position and stare out to where the sea must be.

The river shines silver in the moonlight, the flat stones beneath its surface showing me that it's shallow enough to walk across. And on the other side of the riverbank the pearly darkness of the wood seems to stretch on forever.

12

I shiver as I huddle closer to the fire, the warmth thrown by its flames unable to thaw the freezing core that sits at the heart of me.

Hunched opposite me, Johnny stares blankly into the flames, the shadows dancing across his face unable to hide his haunted expression.

We've left the river far behind. It was too dangerous to try to follow it out of the woods after we both nearly drowned in it. I shiver again as I remember staring into its oil-black depths, the river as deep and wide as an ocean.

We've retreated instead to the trees. Dizzy heaped handfuls of leaves, twigs and broken branches into a rough pile at the heart of this small clearing. At first I didn't think he was going to be able to get the fire to light. I watched him rub two sticks together just like it says you should in *Scouting for Boys*, but he couldn't even get a spark. Then Johnny pulled a lighter out of his pocket. He snapped it open and thrust its flame into the heart of the pile. The fire lit in an instant.

I don't know how the lighter was even working, after the soaking it got. But my clothes are already dry, almost as if they were never wet. I run my hand through my hair, the bandage that was wrapped around my head lost somewhere in the water. Not that it matters—there isn't a wound to protect anymore, not even a scratch.

Nothing makes any sense.

Beyond this circle of flickering light, Dizzy is out there somewhere in the darkness, gathering wood to feed the fire. That's all we can do now. Keep the darkness at bay and wait for morning to come. But as I stare into the flames, I'm not sure I'll ever see the sun rise again.

"Thank you."

Johnny's words are almost lost in the crackling of the fire.

"What did you say?" I ask, uncertain that I've heard him properly.

Looking up, Johnny meets my gaze.

"One second I was standing on the bridge, and the next it was gone and I was in the water."

He flinches as a branch cracks in the fire.

"I was in the water," he repeats, his voice trembling slightly. "I tried to swim, but my legs wouldn't work. I could feel something wrapped around them, dragging me down."

The cold seeps through my veins as I relive the memory. In my mind, I can see the tangled nets wrapped around the legs of the drowning man.

"The waves kept getting higher and higher. It was like the river had carried me out to sea. And I could hear things out there in the darkness. . . ." Johnny's voice trails off. "Terrible things."

My heart thuds in my chest as I remember the sounds I heard as I fought to free the man.

"I shouldn't have been there," Johnny says, his eyes glassy with fear. "I thought I was going to drown. But you saved me."

The fire spits and crackles again, but this time I hear Johnny's words clearly.

"Thank you."

I don't know what to say, so I just nod.

The fire seems to be dying. I look around for something to feed the flames, but the ground has already been scoured clear of sticks. I hope Dizzy comes back soon.

As the flames flicker, the darkness seems to creep closer, and I jump as Johnny speaks again.

"What's happening, Charlie?"

I stare at him in surprise. Johnny never calls me Charlie.

He usually only calls me names that he knows I hate—just like he does to Dizzy. But there's something in his voice that tells me I'm not the only one who's scared of this dark.

I think about the things that I've seen, trying to make sense of the unfathomable. The scattered sticks, the Morse-code call, the sky strange with stars. I don't know what's happening. I'm not sure if this night—this nightmare—will ever end. Maybe we'll be lost in the woods forever.

I shake my head.

"I don't know."

Johnny shudders, almost as if he can hear my private thoughts. Then he starts speaking again, so softly I have to move closer to even catch his words.

"Did you see the man in the water?"

I forget to take a breath, remembering what I saw when I dived beneath the surface. The man in uniform. The drowning man. But it was Johnny I saved from drowning. . . .

For a second, I can't speak, and Johnny seems to take my silence for disbelief.

"There was someone there with me," he continues. "When I was drowning. He spoke to me."

I remember the brass buttons on the man's uniform, shining like tiny suns as he flailed against the dark.

"What did he say?"

"I was swallowing water," Johnny says, his eyes shining brightly as he stares into the flames. "That's when I saw

94

him. It was like my eyes were seeing double. But as I went under, I could hear his voice inside my head. It sounded like an echo of my own, but telling me things I didn't want to hear. About all the things I've done wrong—all the people I've hurt. He told me about the horrors that he'd seen."

I remember the muffled howls I heard above the surface of the water and wonder if that was Johnny. I can tell he's crying now, the tears rolling down his cheeks as he speaks.

"The men on the beaches and the planes diving out of the sky. He said they were sitting ducks, waiting for the boats to come. Bodies in the water. Death everywhere. I was so scared, Charlie. I didn't want to die. Neither of us did. He just wanted to go home—just like me. I made a promise to him—a promise to myself. I said that if I didn't drown, then I'd make things right. All the things I've done wrong, all the people I've hurt—I'd make it all right if he'd just let me live."

From the darkness I hear the crack of a twig snapping underfoot and hope to God this is Dizzy, but Johnny doesn't even seem to hear it as he carries on talking. It's almost as if he can't stop.

"That's when he told me it wasn't my time. There were places I had to go and promises to keep. He said you were coming to save me, Charlie. I just had to call your name."

Johnny looks up to meet my gaze, his eyes bright with tears.

"So that's what I did. I shouted your name with the only

breath I had left. And that's when you came. That's when you saved me."

With a trembling hand, Johnny reaches up to his shirt pocket. "I found this," he says, pulling out a folded square of paper, "when we got out of the water. I swear it wasn't there before. Take a look at it, Charlie."

Reaching out, I take the yellowed paper from his shaking fingers and slowly open it out.

It's a map. In the light cast by the fire, I see the shape of the north of France, the names of cities dotted along the coastline: Boulogne. Calais. Dunkirk. Lines and arrows are drawn across the dog-eared paper, some of them disappearing in the places where the map has cracked at the folds. But it's the words I see scrawled across the English Channel that make me gasp in surprise.

THE WAY FORWARD IS THE WAY BACK

It's the same message we saw written in the Freemasons' code. Inside my head, I see the strange patterns made by the bone-white sticks and remember the laughter echoing from the trees.

"What does it mean?" I breathe, looking into Johnny's eyes and seeing the fear there. "Who wrote this?"

Johnny bites his lip, silent for a moment as he glances out into the dark.

"It's my handwriting," he says, his voice barely more

than a whisper. "But I didn't write this, Charlie. I promise you. It must've been the man in the water."

I stare at the map, the lines and arrows blurring until they look like trees.

"You do believe me, don't you?"

I remember standing in the darkness of the wood as a voice whispered in my ear. I *know* we're not alone here. I fold the map and hand it back to Johnny.

"I believe you."

His face crumples in relief.

"When we get out of here," he says, tucking the map back into his pocket, "I'm going to—"

But whatever Johnny is about to say next is lost as Dizzy stumbles into the circle of light. His arms are empty—he doesn't seem to have found any wood to feed the fire—but his eyes shine bright with excitement as he gestures for us to follow him.

"You've got to see this!"

13

"It's a tree," Johnny says, unable to hide his annoyance at Dizzy dragging us away from the safety of the fire.

I can't help feeling disappointed too as the flashlight beam illuminates the giant oak tree. The fire kept the darkness at bay, but the sickly yellow glow of the flashlight barely touches the shadows as it crawls over the cracks and bulges in the oak's gargantuan trunk.

"I know," Dizzy says, stooping slightly as he directs the flashlight at a darkened crevasse. "It's a really old one too, but look at this."

In the circle of light, the crevasse is transformed into a crude doorway, an opening that time has gouged out of the base of the tree.

A way in.

"Come on," Dizzy says, stooping with the flashlight in his hand as he slips inside the tree. "Follow me."

Ducking my head, I follow Dizzy with Johnny right behind me, both of us eager to stay close to the light. Beyond the doorway the space inside the tree suddenly opens out and we're able to stand up straight again. The smell of old leaves and rotten wood fills my lungs as I take a look around.

"Wow!"

Dizzy props the flashlight in a convenient cranny on the far side of the tree, and as it illuminates the interior, I can see that the tree is completely hollow, the space inside almost big enough to hold most of our class, except maybe Miss James, who'd probably have to duck a bit. Tilting my head, I stare up at a roof of decaying wood and glimpse the tiny beetles crawling there. The air feels warm—so much warmer than the air outside—and my head swims slightly as I step farther inside the tree.

The ground springs beneath my feet, and I look down to see a carpet of ferns. With a sigh of relief, Johnny sinks into the leaves, propping himself up on his elbows as he stretches his legs out.

"We can camp here," he says, the ghost of a smile flitting across his face. "It's safe and warm. When morning comes we can find our way out of the woods."

"That's what I thought," Dizzy says, nodding in agreement. "And that's not all."

He reaches inside the niche where he's propped up the flashlight. For a second, a flickering darkness fills the tree as Dizzy stands in front of the light, but when he turns back round, I can see that his hands are full.

"Look what I found."

The light returns as Dizzy squats down, his flashlight's yellow glow illuminating an array of brightly colored packets as Dizzy spills them onto the floor. Crowding round, we stare at the rainbow of colors now strewn across the bracken. There are chocolate bars, sweets and toffees. It's like Dizzy's been keeping a candy shop hidden away from us.

"Where did you get all these?" Johnny shouts, unable to contain his excitement. "I haven't had anything to eat since lunchtime and you've been carrying around this feast."

Dizzy shakes his head.

"These aren't mine," he says as Johnny tears the wrapper off one of the chocolate bars. "I found them here in the tree."

My stomach twists as Johnny starts to wolf the bar down. I'm just as hungry as he is, but that isn't why I suddenly feel sick.

"Maybe we shouldn't eat these," I say. "Not if they belong to someone else."

"Finders keepers," Johnny replies with his mouth full of chocolate. "Losers weepers."

I look across at Dizzy, who's riffling through the mound of candy. He picks up a chocolate bar and holds it out to me.

"Johnny's right," he says. "If we're going to stay here all night, we've got to have something to eat."

Reluctantly, I take the chocolate bar from Dizzy's hand. On its golden wrapper a single word is spelled out in bright-blue letters: "Secret." But how this stash of sweet things got here isn't a secret—it's a total mystery.

I look again at the brightly colored packets, reading the names written across each one. "Cadbury's Fuse," "Rowntree's Cabana," "Spangles," "Banjo," "Toffo" and "Treets." I don't recognize any of them from the counter of the corner shop.

"This would make a brilliant den," Johnny says as he tears the wrapper off another chocolate bar. "It's warm and dry, and we've got enough food to last for a week." He stretches out on the bed of green bracken that carpets the ground. "This stuff's even comfy enough to sleep on."

It's warm inside the heart of the tree, but that doesn't stop me from shivering. The perfect den filled with treats, but who left them here? Inside my head, I can't help but hear the whisper of a voice in my ear. *Old Crony.*

"This isn't right," I say, dropping the chocolate bar back on the pile as I rise to my feet. "We haven't got time for a midnight feast. We've got to get out of here."

Johnny looks up in surprise.

"What do you want to go back outside for?" he says, unable to hide his horror. "You saw what happened out there."

My eyes dart toward the darkness that lies beyond the doorway. I don't really want to go outside, but we can't stay here either. What if *this* is where Old Crony lives? I take a step toward the place where the flashlight is propped, but as I reach to take it, I feel my foot catch on something hidden beneath the leaves.

Kneeling down to investigate, I touch a sharp edge that tells me straight away that it isn't a tree root. I brush the bracken back to reveal a rectangular wooden box that's been buried beneath the leaves.

"What've you found?" Johnny asks as he and Dizzy crowd round.

The box looks like it's made out of oak, the grain of the wood darkening at the corners and the edges. I open the metal clasp at the front, then lift the lid to reveal a keyboard.

It reminds me of the typewriter I found among Granddad's stuff when I cleared the cupboards out—another piece of post office property that he must have "borrowed" and forgotten to give back. But unlike Granddad's, the typewriter inside this box seems to have two keyboards instead of one.

"It looks like a typewriter," Dizzy says, "but where does the paper go?"

The bottom half of the machine has twenty-six round keys, a different letter of the alphabet shown on each one.

QWERTZUIO

ASDFGHJK

PYXCVBNML

But above this keyboard, where you'd expect the paper to go, the same letters are laid out again, each one contained in a dull flat circle. I try tapping at one of these top letters, but nothing happens.

"It must be broken," Johnny says.

I press one of the bottom keys, feeling it click beneath my finger. As the key clicks, one of the top letters lights up with a bright white light.

"No," I say, glancing up in triumph. "It works."

Johnny shakes his head.

"It's broken."

He points at the letter that's lit up. Instead of the letter "A," which I pressed, the letter "N" is illuminated. Feeling confused, I tap the "A" key again, but this time the letter "G" lights up.

"Must be a loose wire," Dizzy says. "That's why it's getting the letters wrong."

I shake my head. There's something familiar about this machine, the touch of the keys beneath my fingers reminding me of something. Peering more closely, I spot a single word engraved in the wood, almost hidden near the hinge. The small black letters are arranged in the shape of an oval. "ENIGMA," it reads.

I know what this word means. I remember Dad sitting at the kitchen table, his newspaper spread open in front of him as he puzzled over the crossword. "Seventeen down," he barked. "It's the last blasted clue I can't get. 'Something of a mystery.' Six letters. First letter 'E,' second letter 'N,' last letter 'A.'" This was my signal to go scurrying for the dictionary on the shelf near the door. I remember flipping through its pages until I found the words that started with "en," running my finger down the page as I checked their definitions. Dad reckons it doesn't count as cheating if I do this. I remember my finger pausing as I found a word that fitted the clue. "'Enigma,'" I said, reading the definition out loud. "'Something very difficult to understand; a puzzle.' E-N-I-G-M-A." I remember Dad grunting in satisfaction as he filled in this final answer, the flash of his temper postponed for another time.

Sitting in the heart of the tree, I stare down at the strange machine. That's what it is. A puzzle. A mystery. An enigma. But I can't help feeling there's something I'm missing—a fragment of a thought, floating just out of reach at the back of my mind. Not quite a memory, but something I need to know.

Without thinking, I start to move my hands across the

keyboard. The top letters light up one after the other as I tap at the keys.

V	A
C	S
Q	T
P	O
H	R
I	M
J	I
M	S
Z	C
V	O
H	M
Y	I
G	N
B	G

This is important, but I don't know why. With every click of the keyboard, I feel like I'm turning a key, but the riddle still stays firmly locked. My head aches as I try to make sense of the flashing symbols. I'm not even thinking about the keys that I press, but it seems like the same patterns of letters keep lighting up again and again.

ISCOMINGASTORMISCOM
INGASTORMISCOMINGAS
TORMISCOMINGASTORM

Inside the tree the air seems to thicken, the glow of the flashlight now tinted with a strange blue light.

"I don't like this," Johnny says, his voice suddenly loud in my ear. "Something's not right."

I can't answer, keeping my eyes fixed on the machine. My fingers move without asking, tapping at the keys as the lights flash on and off. The air seems to crackle with electricity, almost as if a signal is being sent. Deep inside, something tells me that if I can decode this, then I'll save us all.

"Charlie, stop!" Dizzy says. "You're scaring me."

From somewhere in the distance I hear a rumbling sound, but my fingers keep frantically pecking away. I'm so close to working out what this means.

"Stop it!" Johnny shouts.

But I can't get my fingers to stop as the riddle is unlocked. It's as if this strange machine has taken control of them, the lights behind the letters flashing out the same message that we heard in the bird's Morse-code call.

A STORM IS COMING

Reaching over me, Johnny flips the top of the box, and I have to snatch my hands away before my fingers are crushed by the closing lid.

Feeling dazed, I stare up at him in shock.

"I'm sorry," Johnny says, his face painted with fear in

the strange blue light. "I didn't know how else to get you to stop."

I feel a strange tingling sensation and look down to see the hairs on my arms standing on end.

Then the entrance to the tree is illuminated by a flash of blinding light, instantly followed by a thunderous boom.

And I realize that the storm isn't coming. It's here.

14

"Get out! Get out!" Dizzy shouts, grabbing hold of my arm as another boom shakes the tree.

Blinking, I look through the doorway that's carved out of the trunk, the world outside momentarily lit by another blinding flash. The thunder follows instantly; an earsplitting crack even louder than the last.

I close my eyes against this brightness, the scene outside still illuminated against my eyelids. Inside my head I hear Johnny's singsong voice: *Beware the oak; it draws the stroke.*

Lightning always strikes the highest point, and we're inside a tree.

We've got to get out.

Snatching the flashlight, Johnny pushes past us, ducking his head as he squeezes through the doorway. Dizzy keeps a tight grip on my arm as we follow him, the two of us clambering out into the seething darkness.

Branches crash around us as the storm roars through the forest. I raise my hand to shield my eyes from a swirling blizzard of leaves as another flash of lightning silhouettes the trees.

Inside my head I start counting the seconds before the inevitable roll of thunder.

One Piccadilly, two Piccadilly, three Picca—

BOOM!

The ground shakes as this explosion of sound engulfs us, almost knocking me off my feet.

"Stay away from the trees!" Johnny shouts, his voice almost lost in the tumult. "The lightning can't hit us all if we split up."

He turns on his heel, the flashlight beam flailing wildly as he runs into the raging dark.

Another blinding flash illuminates the shadows, followed almost simultaneously by a thunder crack that rattles my bones. Dizzy lets go of my arm, pushing me forward as the ground heaves again beneath our feet.

"Run!" he shouts.

There's nothing else I can do.

I run.

The woods groan as I dive beneath the whipping branches, the trees contorted as if they're being tortured by the storm. I crash through the undergrowth, my chest heaving as I hurdle over fallen limbs. The air tastes of electricity.

Another blinding flash throws the world into silhouette. Then a tree explodes.

It seems to happen in slow motion. A bright gash of flame splits the trunk, the bark blown off in a shower of shrapnel. The force of the blast knocks me off my feet, pressing my face to the ground as the explosion resounds.

I can smell burning.

I lift my head. The air is filled with smoke and dust, but through the gap now torn in the canopy of leaves, I can see a strange orange glow. It looks like the sky is on fire.

My ears are still ringing, but as I look up at this patch of sky, I see tiny specks of flashing light, incredibly bright against the crimson smoke. And after each flash, I hear another sound above the ringing in my ears, a terrible screaming noise that gets louder with every second that passes. I clap my hands over my ears, burying my face in the fallen leaves as the screams reach a crescendo and the ground shudders again.

This doesn't feel like a storm anymore.

My heart pounds in my chest as I lift my head to see moonbeams raking the sky, each one nearly as bright as daylight. I glimpse the silver shape of a plane caught like a moth in this searching light and hear the angry drone of its engines. Dazed, I watch as the plane disappears into the darkness again, the engine noise swelling to a grinding roar that sounds like a furious swarm of bees. Then another blinding flash illuminates the sky, night turning to day for a split second before darkness falls and a deafening boom thunders through the trees.

This feels like a war.

I scramble to my feet, desperate to escape from this new nightmare. Darkness surrounds me as I plunge into the smoke and dust. Underfoot, twigs crack like gunshots as I run. The shadows of the trees look like ruined buildings, the woods transformed into a shattered city through whose streets I run.

I don't know where Dizzy and Johnny are. I don't even know if they're still alive. But as I run into this choking darkness, I don't think I'll ever see the sun again.

Then I hear it. A shrill whistle somewhere up ahead.

I stumble toward it, my chest heaving as the smoke begins to clear. In the shadowed spaces, I can see mangled branches, now stripped bare of their leaves. Pushing past them, I hear the shrill whistle again, and I pray to God that it's Dizzy.

Then the woods suddenly open into a small clearing and I see the figure of a man standing there.

I freeze.

The man stands with his back to me, his dark-blue overalls almost lost in the darkness as he stares up into a pitch-black sky. For a second, I think it must be the same man I saw under the water, but then I remember that his uniform was browny-green, not blue.

A flurry of dazzling flashes suddenly lights the sky, each one quickly fading to a pinprick of brightness. And then the screaming starts again.

The man turns and starts running, his lolloping stride bringing him straight in my direction as he dives for the cover of the trees. Another boom shakes the ground, and I have to cling to a tree trunk to stop myself from falling down. The world is falling apart and we're the only ones left.

I look down and see the man crouching at the base of the tree. He's rocking back and forth on his heels, the whistle that brought me here hanging on a cord around his neck. His face is hidden beneath the brim of a black bowl-shaped helmet. On the front of it there's a letter "W" painted in white, but what that means I have no idea.

I back away, frightened that this really is Old Crony. But as I do, a stick snaps underfoot and I hear the man moan in terror.

"Make it stop. Make it stop. Make it stop."

His shoulders shake as he sobs, and before I properly realize what I'm doing, I find myself crouching by his side. My heart races as I reach out to rest my hand on his arm.

"It's all right," I say. "You're not alone."

The man lifts his head, his dark-brown eyes opening wide as he stares at me in disbelief.

"Charlie."

I hold my breath, not knowing what to say as I stare back at Dizzy's grown-up face. He looks like he's twenty or thirty years old, the lines around his eyes creased in a world-weary expression. I feel like I'm drowning, the same sensation I felt when I was lost in the water. It's like the world is in two places at once and I can't tell which is real.

"What's happening?" I murmur as the sky lights up again. "Is this still the storm?"

"They call it the—"

A screaming sound drowns out the rest of Dizzy's sentence. His face freezes in fear as the sound gets louder, shifting in pitch from a scream to a whine before a shuddering boom shakes the tree.

I cling to Dizzy's arm to stop myself from falling over.

"They come every night," he says, his hand shaking as he reaches for the whistle around his neck. "Wave after wave of planes, each one louder than the last. The chief warden told me I have to blow this whistle when I hear them—to warn people to take shelter—but tonight the bombs started falling before I had the chance to clear the street."

Tears roll down Dizzy's cheeks as a flash followed by another thunderous boom makes us cringe in terror.

"They've never been this close before," he says, his voice almost lost in the aftershock. "Someone told me you never hear the bomb that's got your name on it, but every time I hear that terrible screaming sound, I think, what if they're wrong?"

The whistle trembles as Dizzy holds it in his hand, his grown-up fingers dark against the shining brass. Meeting his gaze, I see the shadow of the boy he was flicker across his face.

"We should never have left the woods, Charlie. We were safe there."

Feeling confused, I glance at the trees that surround us. Behind their inky branches, I see the ghostly shapes of houses in the gloom. Fear coils around my throat as I remember who lives in the woods.

"This can't be right," I murmur, gazing up at the nearest house. Beneath a sloping roof, darkened windows stare back at me like eyes. "Where are we?"

"London," Dizzy replies as another flurry of dazzling flashes lights up the sky.

Hearing this word, I feel hope surge in my chest. Ever since Dad made us leave the city, I've wished that we could go back. I clamber to my feet and start to run toward the darkened house. I've got to find out if this is real.

"Charlie!" Dizzy calls, his voice hoarse with fear. "Come back! It's not safe!"

But I'm not listening. Under the icy-white light that shines down from the sky, I can see a whole street of terraced houses stretching away into the woods. It looks just like the one we used to live on. I feel like I'm coming home.

"Charlie!"

I'm nearly at the door, the woodland floor turning to steps beneath my feet, when I hear a screaming whine getting louder by the second.

I look up as the noise becomes a roar and realize with a shudder that Dizzy was right: you do hear the one with your name on it.

BOOM!

The sound of thunder lifts me off my feet, slamming me sideways as everything falls. Even the darkness.

15

I can taste dust, thick specks of grit sliding between my teeth as I clench my jaw against the pain. My ears are still ringing, the thunderous sound that I heard before the world fell down around me now stilled to a distant roar.

Forcing my eyes open, I blink in confusion. I can't see a thing. Everything's black, the darkness surrounding me a solid block. I blink again, but nothing changes. It's still pitch-black. Have I gone blind? Maybe I'm dead.

Panicking, I try to move, but something heavy is pinning me down. I can feel broken things beneath me, glass crunching as I shift my weight to find out what they are. I reach up and my fingers touch splinters of wood inches from my face. I move my hand across the surface, feeling the weight of the wood. It seems as broad as a tree trunk, slanting down and trapping me in this darkness.

I push against the timber, but that only sends a fresh shower of dust onto my face. I cough, tasting the grit in my mouth again. Then I push even harder, straining every muscle to try to shift the weight, but the wood just stays where it is. It's no good. It's too heavy for me to move on my own.

I take my hand away, panting heavily as I try to keep the panic from taking me over. Then I hear an ominous creaking and the wood seems to shift, juddering sideways and downward until its splinters scratch at my cheek.

I twist my head away, desperately trying to pull myself free before the whole thing comes down on top of me. Something's still pinning me down, but as I shift my weight, the splintered timber shudders to a stop.

I lie still in the darkness, hardly daring to breathe. Fear catches in my throat, the cloying warmth of this tiny prison wrapping the memory of another moment around me. Closing my eyes, I retreat into this, escaping from the darkness into the warm embrace of my mother's arms. I remember her sitting on my bed, the two of us snuggled beneath a blanket as she read me *The Wind in the Willows*. I can hear her voice in my ear, soft and timid, as she speaks Mole's words aloud.

" 'What lies over *there?*' asked the Mole, waving a paw

toward a background of woodland that darkly framed the water-meadows on one side of the river.

" 'That? Oh, that's just the Wild Wood,' said the Rat shortly. 'We don't go there. . . .' "

I remember Mum hugging me tightly as she raised her voice to drown out the sound of Dad hammering on the door downstairs. His drunken cries pleading with Mum to let him in and warning her what will happen if she doesn't.

That's when I hear something.

I open my eyes, the memory refusing to fade as the darkness swims into view. It sounds like some kind of wild animal, its mewling cry close to me in the absolute gloom.

I stare into the pitch-black, my heart racing as I try to work out what it is. Inside my head I hear Mum's voice, trembling slightly as she lists the animals who live in the Wild Wood.

" 'Weasels—and stoats—and foxes—and so on.' "

I remember the scratchy drawings of these sinister creatures, their claws scurrying across the page. Is that what's out there in the darkness?

The whimpering comes again, almost close enough to touch. Whatever this animal is, it sounds like it's hurt.

Pushing my fear to one side, I reach out toward the source of the sound. My heart thumps in my chest as I brush past dust and debris, the animal's mewling cry guiding my hand in the darkness. Then my heart skips a beat as instead of feeling the fur I expected to find, I touch skin.

I draw back in shock, but the cry comes again, even louder this time.

Tentatively, I trace the shape in the darkness, feeling tiny hands clenched into fists as the cry becomes a howl. Touch and sound combine to shift the picture in my mind. This isn't an animal—it's a baby.

"'And beyond the Wild Wood again?'"

I hear the echo of Mum's voice soft in my ear, still telling me the story as I try to make sense of what's happening here.

"'Beyond the Wild Wood comes the Wide World,' said the Rat. 'And that's something that doesn't matter, either to you or me.'"

Before the world fell down, I felt like I was in two places at once, but now I don't know where I am. I hardly know what's real anymore, but this baby is.

I stroke its head, feeling the warmth and softness of its skin as it carries on crying. It sounds so scared—just like me. Carefully, I place my arm around the baby's body, cradling its head as I draw it close to me.

The baby's wail grows even louder, making me worry that I've hurt it somehow. I can barely see a thing in the darkness, but I feel the baby squirming next to me. I cradle it in my arms, not knowing what to do, as the timber that's trapping us creaks again dangerously.

"Hush," I whisper, frightened that the slightest sound could bring the whole thing down. "Please stop crying."

The baby wails again, its fists drumming against my chest. I hold the baby closer, crooning softly as its mewling cry fills the darkness. Beneath the dust, its skin smells of vanilla, the scent suddenly summoning another memory out of the darkness.

No, not a memory, but some kind of dream.

In my mind, I see moonlight falling across a baby's face, her eyes open wide against the dark. I don't know where this vision has come from, but it seems so real. I watch myself turn away from the window, moonlight spilling through a crack in the curtains as I cradle the baby in my arms. I feel so tired, the empty crib in the corner mocking me with thoughts of sleep as the baby cries out again. I feel myself swaying, gently rocking the baby from side to side as I sing a lullaby.

"Rock-a-bye, baby, in the treetop, when the wind blows, the cradle will rock."

Lying here in the dust and darkness, I sing the same words now as the baby squirms in my arms. Above our heads, I hear the creaking timber start to crack, and cling tightly to the baby, wanting to keep it safe for as long as I can.

"When the bough breaks, the cradle will fall." My voice falters as debris starts to fall around my ears. "Down will come baby, cradle and all."

Then the darkness is peeled back with a thunderous crack, and as light floods in, I glimpse large hands reaching toward me. Screwing my eyes shut against the sudden brightness, I feel myself dragged clear of the wreckage, still clinging to the baby as it wails against my chest.

"Don't worry." The man's voice cracks with emotion as I feel the baby lifted from my arms. "You're safe now."

Opening my eyes, I see the grown-up Dizzy framed by a flickering light. He gently holds the baby against his chest, the gaping facade of a house in ruins burning behind him. As I climb to my feet, he meets my gaze with a grateful stare.

"I'd almost given up hope of finding anything alive. How could a baby survive underneath this mountain of rubble?" Beneath the brim of his black metal helmet, Dizzy's eyes shine with tears as the baby in his arms cries out again. "But then I heard you singing, Charlie. The sound of a lullaby showing me where to find you in the darkness. Just like in the woods."

A sudden flash lights the sky, turning night into day in an instant. Glancing around, I see the world lying in ruins, the fronts torn off terraced houses as piles of bricks and broken timbers spill into the street. Then darkness falls again with a thunderous boom. The woods seem a very long way away now.

Still holding the baby in one arm, Dizzy reaches for the whistle around his neck.

"I didn't understand then," he says, "but it all makes sense to me now." He holds out his whistle toward me. "You need to take this, Charlie."

Another boom shakes the world, even closer now.

My fingers tremble as I reach to take the whistle, its long brass cylinder heavy in my hand. Behind Dizzy, I see bricks begin to crumble and hear the crackling of flames. My mouth feels dry, the taste of smoke and dust sticking in my throat.

"What am I supposed to do?"

Dizzy cradles the baby, its cries filling the sky as the world falls down around us.

"Just blow the whistle and I'll find you again. Things will be better then."

I don't know what Dizzy means, but anything has to be better than this. I close my eyes, shutting out the sight of the falling debris as I raise the whistle to my lips.

And then I blow.

The shrill screech of the whistle cuts through the darkness, its piercing note drowning out all other sounds. It's so loud I think the whole world must be able to hear it, but as I blow, the whistling note seems to twist into a lilting melody.

Rock-a-bye, baby, in the treetop, when the wind blows, the cradle will rock.

My eyes open wide in surprise, the whistle falling from my lips as the lullaby fades into silence.

I look around.

The clearing stands empty, and all I can see are the shadows of the trees.

Dizzy's gone.

"Dizzy!"

My shout echoes in the silence. The ruined buildings, the burning house, the baby crying as Dizzy held it in his arms . . . Everything's gone, and I'm still lost in the woods.

I peer into the darkness, the bare branches of the trees now black against the night. I shiver. It's getting cold, and suddenly I feel very alone.

Then, to the left, I see a fuzzy yellow light moving through the woods.

"Charlie!"

It's Dizzy, calling my name.

"Over here!"

The flashlight beam turns in my direction, the dark shadowed spaces surrounding me suddenly illuminated by pale-yellow light. Dizzy stumbles into the clearing with Johnny following close behind, the flashlight in his hand.

I blink in the sudden glare of its beam.

"Are you all right?" Dizzy asks breathlessly. "We heard the sound of a whistle. I thought it was playing a song." He glances down at the whistle in my hand. "Where did you find it?"

As Dizzy looks up, I meet my friend's gaze, his face unlined by age. Just a boy again.

"You gave it to me."

16

"This time we stick together," Johnny says, his breath fogging the air as he speaks. "Whatever happens."

We're walking side by side, our steps keeping time as we crunch through the leaves. The crisp darkness of the wood stretches ahead of us, shadows seeping through the branches as the track twists again.

I look up.

Not a single leaf remains on the trees. The storm has stripped every branch bare. But deep down I know this wasn't a storm.

I shiver. It's as though the woods have turned from summer to winter in a single night. And it's so cold.

Why is it so cold?

"What time do you think it is?" Dizzy asks through chattering teeth. "Surely it must start to get light soon."

Staring up through the wirework of bare branches, I can see only a glowering darkness, the sky thick with clouds. No chance of spotting the North Star now. No stars to see at all. I remember the climb I made to the top of the tree and what I saw there.

Maybe the woods go on forever. Maybe this night will never end.

"It must," I tell Dizzy, even though I don't know if it's true.

And then I see them. White flakes floating down like feathers through the night. The light from the flashlight catches them, every glistening crystal a falling star. My mouth drops open in surprise and I taste frost on my tongue.

"It's snowing."

The snow is falling straight and steady, a thickening whiteness that quickly turns the path ahead into a blur.

"It can't be snowing," Johnny says, his voice incredulous as we stop and stare. "It's the middle of May."

But the snow doesn't seem to care that it's summertime, the silent flakes shimmering diamond sharp against the dark. There are so many of them. Hundreds, thousands, maybe even millions. The sky is transformed into a forest of flakes, each one an icy splinter slowly drifting to the ground.

I open my hand and watch as one of the snowflakes lands in the center of my palm. Peering closely, I see icy branches leafing out from the middle of its starlike shape. It looks like a forest caught in a single snowflake.

I remember reading once that no two snowflakes are alike. Each snowflake is born in a cloud when tiny ice crystals stick together until they become so heavy that they start to fall to the ground. Any change in temperature or the amount of moisture in the air as they make their journey down gives the snowflake its unique shape.

And then it's gone.

I shiver again, my school uniform offering little protection against this biting cold. Ahead, the drifts of dead leaves have disappeared beneath a fresh white bandage, the track transformed into a carpet of sparkling snow that illuminates the world from below.

"We've got to keep moving," I say, clapping my hands against my arms to try to drive the cold out. "If we stay here, we'll freeze to death."

We press on, wading through the rising snow as the flakes continue to fall. It's almost up to my ankles now, impossible as it seems. The snow smothers every sound, but I can't help feeling that I can hear something else at the very edge of my hearing.

Another tread of footsteps following close behind.

I glance over my shoulder, but I can only see three sets of footprints.

There's nobody following us.

I turn back, wrapping my arms around myself as we walk into this frozen world. I feel the snow crunch beneath my shoes, my feet cutting fresh tracks for anyone to follow. Then I hear an echoing tread, each footstep falling a split second after mine.

Feeling the fear, I glance at Dizzy and Johnny in turn, wondering if they hear it too. But they don't show any sign that they have, their faces set against the falling snow as we breathe out clouds of icy air.

The footsteps are right behind me now.

I stop dead in my tracks and spin round to try to surprise whoever's following us. But the path between the trees lies empty. There's nobody there.

I think I'm going mad.

"Come on, Charlie," Dizzy calls, turning to see where I've gone as Johnny pushes on ahead. "We need to stick together."

Blinking back my tears, I hurry to catch up.

The path is narrowing now, forcing us into single file as it twists through the trees. Even though the snow is still falling, somehow it doesn't seem quite so cold anymore. I peer through the undergrowth that hems us in on both sides, straining to see a way out as the path turns sharply again.

Then I almost crash into Dizzy. My friend is standing stock-still next to Johnny as the path opens into a shadowy glade. I push past to see where we are.

This clearing looks the same as the one we left, a stand of eight trees surrounding us in a tight circle. These trees are ancient, their broad trunks furred with moss while, at the tops, spiky dead boughs rise at strange angles against the darkened sky.

I gaze up through these leafless branches to see the moon shining down, the smoky clouds scudding away as a last few snowflakes drift through this silvered darkness.

"It's another dead end," Johnny says, his voice despairing as he stands by my side. Dizzy joins us there in the center of the clearing, the three of us looking in vain for any way out. But as I stare at the bare trees, I suddenly realize that this isn't another dead end. It's exactly the same one.

"The way forward is the way back," I murmur, the words mocking me as I speak them out loud. I glance down at the ground, the bone-white sticks and pebbles that spelled out the message now buried beneath the snow. It's as though every path we've taken has been bringing us back to this place.

Then I hear the soft crunch of footsteps breaking through the crusty snow.

"Can you hear that?" I whisper, my heart freezing in fear again.

Dizzy shakes his head.

"Hear what, Charlie?"

"There's someone coming," I say, keeping my voice low in case I'm overheard.

The crunching is getting louder, but I can't tell which direction it's coming from. I spin around, searching the trees for any sign of the person who's following us.

"I can't hear anything," Johnny says, his voice sounding as worried as Dizzy's now. "Charlie, are you sure you're all right?"

Crunch. Crunch. Crunch.

"Why can't you hear it?" I ask, panic swelling like a rising tide deep inside me. "It's getting closer."

The shadows cast by the trees reach toward me, and as my eyes flick over them something seems to click inside my mind. My gaze flits up to the stag-headed branches, their shapes silhouetted against the silvery light. I've seen these shapes before. Dazed, I turn round slowly, trying to catch this fleeting memory as it dangles out of reach.

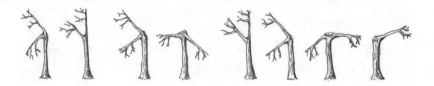

The trees almost look like people, standing with their crooked arms outstretched. I stretch my own arms out, mirroring their shapes as the memory sharpens into view.

"Charlie, what's wrong?"

As well as using Morse code, scouts can use semaphore to send messages. They hold up two flags with their arms stretched out, each letter of the message made by the angles they hold their arms at. I remember standing in my bedroom with Dad's scouting book open on the desk in front of me, my arms stretching into different shapes as I practiced these semaphore signals.

I do the same again now, the world slowly turning as each tree turns into a letter in my mind.

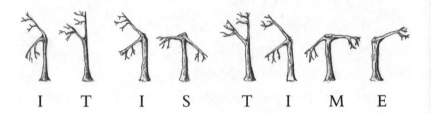

I T   I S   T I M E

"It is time."

As the words leave my mouth, the world seems to stop. Silence fills the woods as a falling snowflake hangs suspended in front of my face. I stare at it in astonishment; the delicate star of snow crystals frozen in the air. I look around to see Dizzy and Johnny are frozen too, Dizzy's hand motionless as it reaches toward me.

Then the silence is broken by the sound of crunching footsteps. My heart thumps in my chest as I turn round to see the dark shape of a man step out of the trees.

He wasn't behind us. He's been ahead of us all the time.

"Hello, Charlie," he says.

17

The man is dressed in what looks like a dark suit, his jacket buttoned up against the cold.

He walks toward me, his footsteps crunching through the fresh snow. As the shadows from the trees fall across his face, the man looks impossibly old, but then he steps again into the moonlight and I see with surprise that he's young, maybe not even twenty years old.

A chill creeps up my spine, the hairs on my neck prickling as the man comes closer still. This is the very heart of the woods, and I know who lives here. I can't stop my voice from shaking as I speak my fear out loud.

"Are you Old Crony?"

The man cocks his head. I struggle to focus as I stare into his fathomless eyes. It's as though he's standing at the very edge of my vision, even though he's right in front of me. My gaze keeps sliding off to the side, his face blurring in a way that makes him look young and old at the same time.

Silence hangs in the air between us, every second that passes feeling like a lifetime to me.

"I have been given many names," he says finally, each word as crisp as snow. "Some used to call me Cronos. But Old Crony seems to fit this place, for now."

I should be more frightened than I am. My very worst fear is standing right in front of me. But I never thought Old Crony would be wearing a suit.

My eyes dart to Dizzy and Johnny again, looking for help, but the two of them just stand there motionless, just like the snowflake that still hangs in the air in front of my nose.

"Johnny says you eat children."

Old Crony smiles in reply.

"Your friend is quite right," he says. "I eat everything in the end."

My heart hammers in my chest.

"You're just trying to scare me," I say, fixing Old Crony with my fiercest glare even though I only want to turn and run. "And Johnny's not my friend."

Old Crony stops in his tracks, his brow furrowing slightly as he faces me in the center of the clearing.

"Oh, but he will be," he replies. "Or he once was. It's

difficult to keep these things in order sometimes. Everything changes, you see. I have watched this land rise from beneath the waves and seen its mountains crumble into dust. I have seen the seas flood in and watched the forests grow until they reach from shore to shore. I was there when your ancestors climbed down from the trees, and I have seen the stars go out across the universe." Old Crony peers up into the silvered sky, twisted boughs rising behind him like antlers from his head. "I think I like the trees the best."

I stare at Old Crony openmouthed. What he's saying makes no sense, but somehow I believe every word.

"Who *are* you?"

Old Crony drops his gaze to meet mine.

"I am Time."

I can't stop myself from laughing out loud.

"That's ridiculous," I splutter. "Time is what you tell from a clock on a wall—it's not a person."

"Look around," Old Crony says, spreading his arms wide as the snowflakes hang suspended. "What time is it now?"

Out of habit, my eyes flick down to my wristwatch, the hands on its face still frozen at half past six. Suddenly that feels like a very long time ago.

"My watch got broken when I fell," I say, my voice faltering as I glance up to meet Old Crony's gaze again. "I can't tell you what time it is now."

"Oh, but that *is* the time," he replies with a knowing smile. "That is always the time. The time is *now*."

His dark eyes glitter in the moonlight, and for a second it looks like they're full of stars.

"But there is no single *now*," Old Crony continues, his voice soft in the hushed silence. "You see the world from the place you are standing, but when you *move*, time and space change too. What is *now* for you may lie in someone else's future, while an event that is just a memory for you may be someone else's *now*. It all depends on where you are looking from and the direction you are traveling."

I stare at Old Crony, struggling to make sense of what he's telling me, but my thoughts feel as frozen as the snowflakes that surround us.

"I'm sorry, but that's impossible," I say, shaking my head to clear my muddled mind. "How can what's happening *now* be in the future or what's happened in the past be someone else's *now*? That's not how things work."

"There is no need to apologize," Old Crony says, reaching out to pluck a snowflake from the air. "It is difficult for you to comprehend. You experience time as something that flows—constantly moving from the past into the future—but that is just a fiction. A story stitched together from an endless succession of frozen moments. Time is not a river but a vast ocean. Every event that has ever happened and every event that ever will happen—not just here on Earth, but all across the universe—exist side by side in an infinity of *nows*. And I can see them all."

I stare at him in confusion, expecting to see the snowflake melt between his fingers, but somehow it stays frozen in his grasp. I watch as Old Crony lifts it to his lips and then, with a soft puff of breath, sends it soaring into the air.

"A man called Albert Einstein once said," he continues, "or will say—it's hard for me to remember exactly which now—that the distinction between past, present and future is only a stubbornly persistent illusion. The laws that govern the universe do not care which way time flows. If time suddenly started flowing backward, from the future into the past, then this world would keep spinning around the sun."

I look up in astonishment as I watch every snowflake that has hung suspended in the air suddenly start to rise, a flurry of ice crystals falling upward into the darkness. Next to me, I hear Dizzy and Johnny start to move, and I turn toward them in the hope that they've broken free of whatever force has been keeping them frozen.

But their eyes stare straight ahead as they begin to walk backward through the clearing. The snow crunches beneath their feet as they trace their steps in reverse, each footprint erased. The sight is so strange that it makes my head hurt. I watch as the two boys disappear into the trees, leaving me alone with Old Crony.

I turn back to him. Nothing makes any sense. Nothing's made any sense from the second I hit my head.

"I don't understand."

Old Crony stares at me, his gaze suddenly terrifying.

"You people chase time, you waste time, you borrow time and you lose time. You say time flies, time heals and time will tell. You are in time, you are on time, you have all the time in the world and then you're out of time, but you never really understand what time is. You are blinded by the moment in which you live, but you fail to realize that each passing moment contains both its future and its past. Can't you see that now, Charlie?"

My head spins with thoughts of all the things that I've seen. The man in the water and a sky filled with fire. All constellations gone as the woods stretched on forever. Mum and Dad arguing, the strange typewriter hidden inside the tree, a baby crying as the world lay in ruins. I think about what Old Crony has told me, but when I try to speak, the words seem to catch in my throat.

"All the things I've seen tonight," I ask, fighting back tears. "Are they glimpses of the future or the past? I don't know what any of this means."

In reply, Old Crony takes a step toward me and gently rests his hand on my shoulder.

"Every life is a series of moments," he says. "That is what you have glimpsed. Moments in time." I feel the warmth spread from his fingers, driving the cold from my bones. I look at his face, his expression now as calm as a waveless sea. "The future is shaped by the decisions you make, and the actions *you* take will change the world."

Old Crony's words take a second to sink in.

"How can *I* change the world?" I ask, shaking my head in disbelief. "I'm only eleven years old."

"I can see the whole of you, Charlie," replies Old Crony, "stretching through time—all that you have been and the versions of you still to come. You will be so many different people, but somehow remain the same. Perhaps it is only when you look back that you'll be able to make sense of this. But you *will* change the world, Charlie. All you need is time."

The sudden flapping of wings turns both our heads to the sky. I watch as a bird flies backward through the air, its wings beating in reverse, before it lands on the topmost branch of the nearest tree. The small brown bird hops from foot to foot on this leafless perch, the gray-white feathers of its chest puffed up against the chill. I recognize it straightaway, the same bird I saw in the pages of Dizzy's notebook.

It's a nightingale.

Perched overhead, the bird peers down at us with black beady eyes, twitching its tail as if thinking of taking flight again. Then it opens its beak wide, and I hear the nightingale sing.

"This is time," Old Crony says as a rich stream of

whistles and trills pours out of the bird. "Every note of this bird's song is a frozen moment. You only ever hear a single note at a time, but your brain turns it into song. As one note fades into memory, your mind anticipates the next. You are trapped in a now, but you still hear the music."

Silhouetted against the silvered sky, the nightingale quivers as it sings a long, drawn-out note, the sound filling the clearing.

"The song of time lives inside your mind, Charlie. It is your memories, the good and the bad. It is your dreams for the future and the fears that you hide."

I can feel the tears running down my face; the nightingale's song almost too beautiful to bear. My mind is filled with more questions than answers, but there's only one thing I can ask now.

"Why me?"

Lifting his hand from my shoulder, Old Crony softly taps the side of my head.

"You were here and I was passing," he replies with a gentle smile. "Time lives inside your mind. When you fell and hit your head, you caught a glimpse of its great ocean, and now it is time for you to find the farthest shore."

He glances toward the tree where the nightingale is still singing.

"There's someone you have to meet."

Beckoning me, Old Crony starts walking toward the tree. Not wanting to be left behind, I hurry to follow him, the snow crunching beneath my shoes in time with the nightingale's song.

Resting his hand against the gnarled tree trunk, Old Crony turns to me.

"This tree may look old, but it is only a fleeting moment in the universe. Once upon a time it was a seed, then a sapling and, in another time and place, it will be something else again, its wood used to make a floorboard or maybe even a door."

He pushes the trunk and I gasp in surprise as it suddenly swings inward, revealing a perfect rectangle of darkness.

An open door.

"Follow me," Old Crony says, and then he steps into the darkness.

I stand stock-still for a second, feeling my heart thump in my chest. Then, taking a deep breath, I follow Old Crony through the door.

18

For a second I think everything is still covered in snow, the room I find myself standing in completely white beneath the soft lights. But then I realize that it's just the color scheme, the furniture matching the clean white walls. A white chair and sofa are tucked against one wall, while on another, long white curtains are drawn against the night. And in front of me I can see a bed, spotless white sheets covering the figure of the old woman lying there, a snow-white bandage wrapped around her head. I think she's asleep.

I take a step back, feeling like an intruder. But as I move, my shoes squeak against the polished floor and I see a woman turn and step forward from the corner of the room. Her white-and-blue uniform was keeping her camouflaged, the open cupboard behind her filled with soft white towels, but as she stares at me quizzically, I realize that she's a nurse.

"Visiting time doesn't start until nine," she says, keeping her voice low so as not to wake the woman in the bed. "I'm afraid you'll have to leave."

I look around for Old Crony, thinking he'll be able to explain why we're here. But the rest of the room stands empty. Old Crony is nowhere to be seen.

The nurse frowns, mistaking my silence for insolence.

"If you don't leave now, I'll have to call—"

But I don't hear who the nurse is planning to call, as another voice cuts across her.

"This is my great-granddaughter," the old woman says, raising her head from the pillow. "I've been waiting a long time to see her again."

The nurse looks down at her patient, then back at me before glancing at her watch with a tut.

"Just this one time," she says finally. "But don't go tiring yourself out—it's only half past six in the morning, and you need to rest after your fall."

Fussing with the pillows, she helps the old woman up into a sitting position. The woman's nightdress is as white as the sheets that are drawn up to her chest.

"Ten minutes," the nurse says, casting me a warning glance as she walks out of the room. Then the door clicks shut behind her, leaving me alone with the old woman.

She beckons me closer.

"Don't be afraid."

I walk toward the woman, the polished floor squeaking beneath my feet once again. I don't feel scared, just completely confused. This can't be my great-grandmother. Both of mine died before I was born. On the bedside cabinet I see a get-well card standing open next to the envelope it came in. My heart skips a beat as I read the name on the front.

Charlotte Noon.

I look down at the old woman's face. From underneath the bandage, her long white hair fans around her head like a halo of snow. Her pale skin seems shriveled, dark spots and wrinkles marking it like an ancient map. But as I stare into the brightness of her sunken eyes, I see my own eyes staring back.

"You're me," I breathe.

The lines around the old woman's mouth crease as she smiles. The exact same smile I practice in the mirror every day.

"I was," she says. "Or you will be. It's like Old Crony says: it all depends on where you're looking from."

I can't speak, my mind rebelling as I stare at the old woman's face. This can't be me.

"It's OK," the old woman says, reaching out to take my hand. "I always knew this moment would come because I remember it so vividly. But I realize it must be a shock for you now. I remember how shocked I felt then. It's strange for me to see you with these eyes, when it seems like only yesterday I was standing there staring at me."

As she holds my hand, I can feel the bones beneath her papery skin. They feel so fragile, like a small bird's. But as I stare into her eyes, my mind starts to erase the lines I can see there, revealing my own face.

"These wrinkles are just a disguise," the woman says, as though she can read my mind. With her other hand, she reaches up to tap the side of her head, the bandage there reminding me of the one that was wrapped around mine. "I'm still you in here."

Old Crony said there was someone that I had to meet, but I didn't realize it was me.

"I remember every moment of that night so well," Charlotte says. "Those moments seem so close to me now. Johnny chasing us through the woods dressed like some old scarecrow. Falling and hitting my head so hard that I thought my brains would fall out. I remember climbing to the top of the tree and swimming through the river. I can still feel the snow crunching beneath my feet as we walked endlessly through the trees. I thought we'd never get out of those woods."

My eyes fill with tears as the memories come rushing in.

"I'm still lost in the woods."

"I know," Charlotte says, gently squeezing my hand. "I remember how lost I felt back then. Not just in the woods, but all the time."

I see the tears sparkling in her eyes, perfect reflections of mine.

"I know you just want Mum and Dad to stop arguing all the time. But it's not your fault that they do. I remember sitting up in that tiny bedroom night after night, tapping out messages with Granddad's Morse key. All I wanted was to get a message in reply telling me there was a way out. That life could be different somehow."

I nod, remembering staring at the silent Morse key on my desk, waiting for a message that never came.

"When they brought me to this hospital after I fell and hit my head, I knew that the time had finally come," Charlotte says, her voice cracking slightly under the strain. "That I'd get this one chance to see you now—to tell you that it *will* be."

I feel her fingers tap against mine.

"There is a way out of the woods."

In my head, my brain translates the Morse-code taps. *Dot—dash—dot.* Message received.

I remember what Old Crony told me as we stood in the clearing. *The actions you take will change the world.* That's what I need to know now.

"What do I have to do?"

"You need to be brave, Charlie," she says. "Braver than

you think you can ever be. There are dark times ahead—maybe even the darkest. Another war, even worse than the last. There will be times when you think all hope is gone, but never despair. The sun will rise in the end." I feel her hand tighten around mine. "You can't stop what's coming, but you can help to shape it into something better. It's like Old Crony said: you build the future with every action you take, no matter how small. You're good at solving puzzles, Charlie. Think about all these codes you've cracked tonight. Keep on helping Dad with his crossword. These moments all matter in the end."

I stare at my older self, incredulous.

"Is that all you can tell me? That there's a war coming and I have to keep on doing crosswords? How's that going to help me change the world?"

"Words matter," Charlotte replies. "They told us that at Bletchley Park. Finding the right words at the right time can help win a war. The codes you solve will save so many lives, Charlie. There's so much I could tell you, but you need to discover it for yourself. Old Crony told me that time is like an ocean, and I've swum from shore to shore. I have seen kindness and courage and beauty and wonder—oh, there is so much wonder in the world. There may be dark times ahead, but my life—your life—*our* life—is filled with so many moments of happiness. Dancing and laughter and long walks in the park." She looks up at me with an impish smile. "There's even some kissing."

I can't stop myself from blushing, and I see the same pinkness spreading across Charlotte's cheeks. I look down at my future self, her long white hair drifting across the pillow, and the words slip out of my lips before I even realize I'm asking the question out loud.

"Do I have to grow my hair?"

Charlotte's smile widens into a grin.

"One day, maybe," she says. "It's up to you to choose. Everything is possible. You have all this ahead of you. The future is yours to write."

She gives my hand a final squeeze and then lets it go.

"Could you open the curtains for me, Charlie?" she asks, her voice wavering slightly. "I think I'd like to watch the sun rise."

I walk to the window and pull open the long curtains. The room looks out over darkened fields, and in the distance I see a solid line of trees, faint smudges of pink starting to swell above the horizon.

I turn back to Charlotte, her gaze fixed on the distant woods.

"Thank you," she says, her voice even quieter than before.

I go back to the bed and take her hand in mine. My hand. Her breathing seems to slow as together we look out through the window.

The sun is rising above the trees, filling the sky with light. The color changes from pink to orange to a blinding golden glow. It's all happening so fast it seems like time is speeding up.

How many times have I watched the sun rise?

I take a breath and exhale. I don't know whose eyes I'm looking through anymore. But our eyes are the same. We're the same person, caught in two moments in time. No. One moment. This moment. Now.

The world is getting lighter, a new day rising with the dawn.

I take another shallow breath, but the sunrise looks so beautiful I forget to take the next.

The light begins to bleed and I feel myself falling, falling like an arrow into the light.

And then the light is all that I can see.

19

The first thing I hear is a bird singing, the soft fluting notes of its song rising and falling in time with the beat of my heart. The melody sounds so simple at first, the same whistling refrain repeated over and over again. But then I hear another trilling song, a sweet, high sound that swells to fill the spaces left behind by the first.

Another bird starts to sing, and another and another and another. Whistles and warbles, chirrups and tweets, flurries of notes falling like rain inside my brain. The sound seems to be coming from all around, every bird singing at once, their melodies twisting and twining until my mind is filled with an ocean of song.

Then I hear Dizzy's voice calling my name.

"Charlie!"

I open my eyes to see a brilliant light shining through the leaves.

"Wake up," Dizzy says, gently shaking my arm before I slowly pull myself up to a sitting position. "Johnny thinks he's found the way out."

I look around. The room has gone, the old woman who was me nowhere to be seen. I'm sitting in the shade of a large oak tree, rays of light rippling across a wooded glade. There's no snow on the ground, only a carpet of wild-flowers that shine in the pale sunlight. Apart from Dizzy, the clearing is empty. No sign of Old Crony.

I'm back in the woods, but the night has ended.

It's morning now.

"Come on," Dizzy says, gesturing for me to follow him. "It's this way."

Clambering to my feet, I hurry to follow Dizzy as he leads us between the trees. Above our heads the birds are still singing in full voice, but when I glance up I can't see a single bird—only glimpses of blue scattered across a sky of green. It seems almost impossible. Every tree is in full leaf, no sign of the storm that we lived through last night.

"Over here!"

Johnny is standing on top of a bank at the edge of the woods, the spaces between the trees offering a glimpse of the sun as it rises in the sky. Scrambling up the bank to join him there, I rest my hand against a tree trunk as I stare out at the world beyond the woods.

Beneath a brightening sky lies a patchwork quilt of fields painted green and gold in the morning light. A farmhouse is set down in the middle of the fields, but beyond that I can see the village, the roofs of the shops and houses laid out on the horizon, while to the north the squat shape of the church tower rises above the trees.

Johnny and Dizzy scramble down the bank to reach the rutted track that leads the way back. Trying not to slip on the dew-soaked bluebells that carpet the slope, I follow them down, until the three of us are standing together in the sunlight.

We look at each other, almost unable to believe that we've made it out of the woods.

It's Johnny who speaks first.

"We don't say a word about what happened here," he says, the tone in his voice brooking no argument. "Not to anyone. We just say we got lost in the woods and had to camp out all night."

Dizzy nods.

"Nobody would believe us if we did. They'd think we were making it all up. Or put us in the madhouse."

The two boys turn to me, waiting for my reply. I remember watching them walking away, retracing their steps in reverse before disappearing into the darkness. But we can't go backward now.

"What do you think, Charlie?" Dizzy asks.

"Maybe you're right," I say, squinting as I glance up at

the rising sun. "Maybe we can't tell anyone about what happened to us, but that doesn't mean it didn't happen."

I think about what Old Crony told me. Everything changes. And that means we can change too.

"We don't have to be like we were before," I say. "We don't have to be shy or frightened or angry or mean. We can be what we want to be." I look up at Johnny, the sunlight slanting across his face. "We can be friends."

Johnny stares at me before glancing at Dizzy. Then he spits on his palm and holds his hand out for mine.

"Friends." He nods. "All of us."

I shake his hand and then watch as Dizzy does the same.

We grin at each other. The world changed in a moment.

"Come on," Dizzy says. "It's time to go home."

The birds are still singing as we start walking down the track. In the distance the village begins to sharpen into view, and if I squint I think I can even make out the roof of my house, my attic window glinting in the sunlight.

I think about Mum and Dad waiting for me there and the mountain of trouble that I'm in, but the funny thing is I don't feel scared anymore. I've decided to be brave instead.

Glancing down at the track, I catch sight of a newspaper, folded in half and left by the wayside. It must've been dropped by the paperboy who delivers to Jukes's farm.

I stoop down to pick it up. It's a copy of the *Times*, the front page filled with the usual boring list of births, marriages and deaths.

"What've you got there?" Dizzy asks.

"Today's paper," I reply, pointing to the date at the top. Tuesday, May 16, 1933.

"I wonder if there's anything in there about us?" Johnny asks. "Three kids missing in the woods?"

I flip through the pages of newsprint, reading the headlines as they flutter past. LEAGUE OF NATIONS RESOLUTIONS. ANTI-GERMAN BOYCOTT IN AMERICA. THE TENSION IN EUROPE.

In my mind, I hear the echo of my own voice telling me there are dark times ahead. I think about what we saw back there in the woods. Moments in time, but this time is ours. Here and now.

"No," I say, folding the paper back in two. "But there will be. We made it through the woods. We can do anything now. We can change the world."

Tucking the paper beneath my arm, I smile at my friends and we keep walking into the future.

Corporal Johnny Baines of the Royal Army Medical Corps served as a medical orderly with the British Expeditionary Force sent to defend France against German attack at the outbreak of the Second World War. When German forces invaded in May 1940, Johnny's unit was forced to retreat to Dunkirk, a port in the north of France, joining the thousands of Allied troops stranded there. Completely surrounded and coming under heavy attack, more than three hundred thousand soldiers were eventually rescued from the beaches of Dunkirk by a hastily assembled fleet of nearly a thousand boats and ships. As the evacuation took place, Johnny was one of the brave volunteers who remained behind to care for the wounded and the dying, but on the evening of Sunday, June 2, he was ordered to leave his post and join the evacuation. He was picked up by a small fishing boat, but this vessel came under attack on the voyage back to Britain, forcing the crew overboard. As the fishing boat sank, Johnny was caught in its nets and drowned. He was eighteen years old.

In September 1940, Dylan "Dizzy" Heron began studying under a scholarship at the Hornsey School of Arts and Crafts in Crouch End, London, but on the evening of September 7, the Blitz began. This name came from the German word *Blitzkrieg,* meaning "lightning war." London was bombed every day and night for the next eleven weeks. One-third of the city was destroyed, and thousands were left dead or injured. Dizzy volunteered as an air raid warden, helping people to shelters and patrolling to watch for falling bombs. He was awarded the George Medal for his brave actions on the evening of Sunday, October 13, when he rescued an entire family from a house that had suffered a direct hit. Hearing screams, Dizzy ran into the bombed house and dragged three people to safety, before returning to the collapsing building to save a baby who'd been buried beneath the wreckage. After the war, Dizzy worked as a writer and illustrator of children's books, with his best-known novel, *The Nightingale in the Woods,* telling the story of a girl who discovers a magical world. He was made a Member of the Most Excellent Order of the British Empire (MBE) for his services to children's literature and spent the last years of his life campaigning to save the woods near his home, which lay in the path of a planned road scheme.

Charlotte Noon won first prize in a cryptic crossword competition set by the *Daily Telegraph* newspaper in January 1942 and subsequently received a letter from a high-ranking officer in the British army inviting her to London to discuss a matter of national importance. After signing the Official Secrets Act, she was recruited to the Government Code and Cypher School and sent to work at Bletchley Park. There, a host of top mathematicians and problem solvers had been assembled to crack the enemy's secret codes. To encrypt their communications, the Axis powers used the Enigma machine, a device that resembled a typewriter, which turned the text of messages into a series of seemingly random letters, allowing them to be transmitted in Morse code without fear of detection by the Allied forces. When these encrypted messages were received, an Enigma machine could also be used to decode the messages back into readable text. At Bletchley Park, Charlotte joined the team in Hut 8, who were tasked with cracking the Enigma code. Working long hours to decipher enemy messages, they saved countless lives. From predicting which cities German bombers would target in the Blitz to protecting Atlantic convoys bringing in vital supplies from U-boat attack, the cracking of the Enigma code led to discoveries that changed the course of the Second World War. After the war, Charlotte worked for the Met Office, developing mathematical models and computer programs to produce more accurate weather forecasts. In the later part of her career, she pioneered research into climate change, traveling the world with her family in the course of her work. She died at the age of ninety-six after a short illness following a fall at home. Her friends always called her Charlie.

The Science of
The Longest Night of Charlie Noon

From secret codes to the mysteries of time itself, here's more about the real-life science in *The Longest Night of Charlie Noon*.

Can we do this whole thing in code?

-. --- (That's "No" in Morse code.) However, if we were going to use a code to communicate, then Morse code would be perfect. Invented by Samuel Morse in 1838, Morse code assigns a unique combination of dots and/or dashes to every letter in the alphabet. Using electrical pulses, these dots and dashes can be transmitted via telegraph wires or by radio waves to send messages over long distances.

How did people crack the code?

Telegraph operators translated the messages they sent into the Morse-code signaling alphabet and those they received into English letters. Some telegraph operators became so skilled at Morse code that they could work out what a message said just by listening to the clicking of the telegraph. Samuel Morse designed the code so that the most frequently used letters could be entered with the least effort. For example, the letter "E" is coded as a dot and the letter "T" as a dash.

How can I solve this secret message I've been sent?

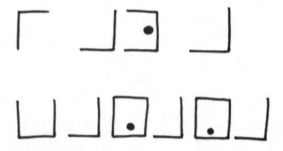

In *The Longest Night of Charlie Noon*, Johnny shows Charlie and Dizzy the Freemasons' code, also known as the pigpen cipher, and that is what this message has been sent in. It was given this name because the grids look like a drawing of the pens where farmers would keep their pigs!

To work out what this message means without cheating and looking back at chapter seven, here's what you need to do.

You can see that the message seems to be four words long, with two of the words in the first line being single-letter words. There are only two single-letter words in the English language—"a" and "I"—so we can guess that the first word of the message might be "A" and the third word "I" or the first word "I" and the third word "a." Let's take a look at the other words for more clues.

The second word starts with the same symbol as the third word, and the fourth word includes this symbol three times. We could try dropping the letter "a" in here to see if this helps us understand the message.

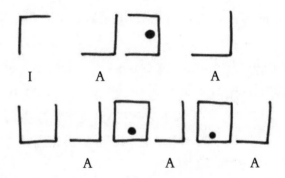

Looking for patterns in secret codes can help you to identify frequently used letters like "A" and "I," and you can then use these to help you to decode the rest of the message. For example, there are not many words in the English language with the pattern "_A_A_A."

I AM A BANANA!

Are you? That's very strange.

159

No, that's what the code says! I've worked it out.

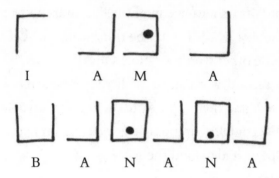

Well done. This kind of code-breaking is called *pattern analysis*.

Another technique for solving a cipher is called *frequency analysis*. This means using knowledge about which letters are most commonly found in words to help crack the code. For example, the most common letters found in words in the English language are "E," "T," "N," "O," "R," "I," "A" and "S," while the least common letters are "Z," "Q" and "X." The letter found most often at the beginning of a word is "T," while the most common last letter of a word is "E." Take a look at the following coded message:

XLMW MW E WIGVIX GSHI

This coded message has used a *substitution cipher,* in which new letters have been substituted for the original letters of the uncoded message. In this case, each letter of the original message has been moved along four places in the alphabet. This is called the *Caesar Shift*, after its inventor, the Roman emperor Julius Caesar. If you move each letter back four places in the alphabet, the message reads:

THIS IS A SECRET CODE

Discovering the rule that has been used to create the code is the key to deciphering it.

But what if I want to create a code that nobody can crack?

Lots of people have tried to create unbreakable codes. Shortly after World War I, a German engineer named Arthur Scherbius invented the Enigma machine. This machine, which looked like a typewriter in a box, used a set of rotors to change the text of any message typed into the keyboard. The rotors could be swapped around and connected in different ways so that every time a key was pressed, another part of the machine transposed pairs of letters. Messages encrypted by an Enigma machine were almost impossible to crack, as the machine had 158,962,555,217,826,360,000 different settings. If you wanted to crack the code by trying out a different setting every second until you found the right one, this would take you five trillion years!

Almost impossible?

During the Second World War, a British code breaker named Alan Turing designed a machine for breaking the Enigma codes. This machine worked by electronically testing different possible keys for the messages fed into it. The ticking of the machine's rotors as they copied the Enigma's encryption technique gave the machine its name: "the bombe." As Turing improved the bombe, the Enigma codes could be cracked in just a couple of hours.

From five trillion years to a couple of hours! That's a big time difference!

But according to Einstein's Special Theory of Relativity, time speeds up and slows down according to the speed at which you are moving. He proposed a famous thought experiment called the twin paradox to help explain this. In this, one twin sets off in a spaceship traveling near the speed of light, while the other twin stays at home. Because time passes more slowly for someone traveling near the speed of light relative to—that means compared to—someone standing still, the trip would only take a couple of hours for the twin on the spaceship, but for the twin left behind on planet Earth, many years would pass before the spaceship returned. As Old Crony says, when you move, time and space change too.

But I still don't understand how this means an event in my future could be in someone's past?

It is complicated, but don't worry! Einstein came up with another thought experiment to help you. Imagine you're standing still on a train platform and another person is standing in the middle of a moving train. As the train speeds through the station, you see two lightning bolts simultaneously striking the front and back of the train at the precise moment you face the person standing in the middle of the train. For you, standing still on the platform, the light from these lightning bolts travels the same distance to reach you at the same time. However, for the person standing in the middle of the moving train, they see the lightning strike the front of the train first because this light reaches them first as they are traveling toward it. Saying when something happens depends on your perspective.

So it's all to do with the speed of light?

Yes, the speed of light is a universal constant, meaning it stays the same—299,792 miles per second—whether the source of light is moving or standing still. For example, if the train is traveling at 100,000 miles per second and turns its headlights on, the beams of light won't be traveling at 399,792 miles per second (the speed of the train + the speed of light) but will still only be traveling at 299,792 miles per second. That's still really fast!

When I look up at the North Star, how long has that light taken to reach me?

The North Star or Pole Star is the name commonly given to Polaris, a star in the constellation of Ursa Minor. Astronomers estimate that Polaris is 433 light-years from Earth. This means when you look up at Polaris, the light you see has taken 433 years to travel from the surface of the star and across the depths of outer space until it finally reaches your eyeball and is absorbed.

Wow, that's a long journey!

It looks like a long journey from here on Earth. But time slows and space shrinks the faster you go, and when you get closer to the speed of light these numbers approach zero. So from the viewpoint of the light, the journey has been instantaneous. It is as if time does not exist.

Now that you've read all about this, the most important thing to know about time is that you should use it wisely. I hope you use your time to help build a better world.

Acknowledgments

"What then is time? If no one asks me, I know what it is. If I wish to explain it to him who asks, I do not know."

So wrote Saint Augustine of Hippo more than 1,500 years ago, but I'd like to thank the authors of the following books for helping me to explore my own questions about time: *The Order of Time* by Carlo Rovelli, *Time Travel* by James Gleick, *Your Brain Is a Time Machine* by Dean Buonomano, *Time* by Eva Hoffman, *Relativity: A Graphic Guide* by Bruce Bassett and Ralph Edney, *Time and the Conways* by J. B. Priestley, *Ammonites and Leaping Fish* by Penelope Lively, *The Voice That Thunders* by Alan Garner, *Four Quartets* by T. S. Eliot, *Fragments* by Heraclitus, and *Pieces of Light* by Charles Fernyhough. As Old Crony says, the song of time lives inside your mind, so I'd also like to thank Kate Bush for her wonderful songs exploring time, memory and the moments that matter.

The writer Robert Macfarlane has spoken of the importance of reconnecting young people with the natural world, and I'd like to thank the authors of the following books for showing me the way into the woods: *The Wild Places* by Robert Macfarlane, *Woodlands* by Oliver Rackham, *Wildwood: A Journey Through Trees* by Roger Deakin, *Oak and Ash and Thorn* by Peter Fiennes, *The Ash and the Beech* by Richard Mabey, *Gossip from the Forest* by Sara Maitland, *Badgerlands* by Patrick Barkham, and *The Lost Words* by Robert Macfarlane and Jackie Morris. I'd also like to make a special mention of the author, illustrator and naturalist Denys Watkins-Pitchford, who wrote under the pen name BB, for the inspiration I found in his timeless writings about the natural world, especially his novel *Brendon Chase*, which in some ways this story is a strange tribute to.

Huge thanks to the Society of Authors' Foundation for the grant they provided to support my research for this novel, and to Gloucestershire Wildlife Trust for the sterling work they do managing Lower Woods, where the novel is set. I'd also like to thank my fantastic agent, Lucy Juckes, and my wonderful editor, Kirsty Stansfield, for all their support and advice. Thank you too to Fi, Catherine, Nicola, Hester, Rebecca, Kate, Ola, Michela, Tom, Julia and all the team at Nosy Crow, as well as Beverly Horowitz and Rebecca Gudelis at my wonderful US publisher, Delacorte Press.

Finally, I'd like to thank my family for all their love, support and understanding. Thank you to my mum and my brother for helping me through the woods when I was growing up, and to my wonderful wife and children for helping me to see the sunlight through the trees.

Charlie, Dizzy and Johnny only live in the pages of this story, but their characters have been inspired by the bravery of countless people who helped to build a better world. Nobody gets to choose the time in which they live, but, as Old Crony says, we shape the future with every action we take. Keep reading and change the world.

About the Author

CHRISTOPHER EDGE grew up in Manchester, England, where he spent most of his childhood in the local library, dreaming up stories. He now lives in Gloucestershire, where he spends most of his time in the local library, dreaming up stories. His award-winning novel *The Many Worlds of Albie Bright* was named a Best Children's Book by the New York Public Library and was nominated for the prestigious CILIP Carnegie Medal in the UK, as were his novels *The Jamie Drake Equation* and *The Infinite Lives of Maisie Day*.

christopheredge.co.uk